A LITTLE LOVING

Jenny Holden fell in love with Matt Chambers, the local high school football star. When she fell pregnant, he didn't believe the baby was his. Now a pro player, he is back in town to attend the wedding of his best friend, who is also Jenny's boss. And when he sees Jenny's son Sam, the boy's parentage is unquestionable. Jenny, now a widow, knows all Sam wants is a father — his real father. But can she trust the man who once turned his back on them?

*Books by Gael Morrison
in the Linford Romance Library:*

PASSION OF THE DRUMS
HEART OF A WOMAN
LOVERS NEVER LIE
MEET ME AT MIDNIGHT
TAKE ME, I'M YOURS

GAEL MORRISON

A LITTLE LOVING

LINFORD
Leicester

First published in Great Britain in 2014

First Linford Edition
published 2016

A catalogue record for this book is available
from the British Library.

ISBN 978–1–4448–2767–5

Published by
F. A. Thorpe (Publishing)
Anstey, Leicestershire

Set by Words & Graphics Ltd.
Anstey, Leicestershire
Printed and bound in Great Britain by
T. J. International Ltd., Padstow, Cornwall

This book is printed on acid-free paper

Dedication

For Vivian

1

With a groan, Jenny Holden banged her palm onto her clock, stopping the ringer before it got started. She didn't want Sam to hear it, didn't want her son up. Not now. Not yet. Not today of all days.

She needed a bath and she wanted it in peace, didn't want to argue with Sam over nothing. She particularly didn't want her son asking questions. She couldn't face that today, not on Jake and Mel's big day.

Jake had done well proposing to Mel. Their wedding would be wonderful, a day to remember, unlike the subdued affair her own wedding had been. Now if only Seattle's crazy weather co-operated.

Jenny listened, but couldn't hear the sound of water flooding down the drain pipes outside her bedroom window or the sound of cars swishing through puddles on the road outside. It had rained in the night, but it wasn't raining now. Thank heavens for that as Jake's wedding was outside.

She twitched open the curtain at the head of her bed. Not a cloud in the sky. As long as the flowers in the Country Club's planters hadn't had their petals blown off in the rain, everything would be beautiful. Her own garden was still filled with blowsy summer blooms, but her yard faced south and retained the heat. It wasn't susceptible to northwestern squalls.

Jenny had warned Jake, her best friend and boss, that if he wanted certainty with regards to the weather, he and Mel should elope to Mexico for the wedding. Jake had replied that weather didn't matter. All he and Mel cared about was that their family and friends would be there.

Two hundred of them according to the invitation list, and almost all were able to attend. There had been no such numbers when Jenny married Phil, just her and Phil's parents, her toddler son Sam, and Jake coming along as moral support. It had been a short ceremony at City Hall, then dinner afterwards at the Ming Court Restaurant.

No drama, no fanfare, and none of the passion that had marked her life before Sam was born. Which had suited Jenny fine. She'd had enough passion and the pain that went with it to last a lifetime.

But she couldn't lie in bed thinking of the past. She still had Jake and Mel's present to wrap. Nothing big, nothing fancy, but something they'd like; two elegant pewter champagne flutes, whose warm metal would keep the liquid inside cool.

She flung back her covers and swung her legs from the bed, then snatched up her dressing gown and tied the cord tight. She tiptoed down the hall towards the kitchen. Coffee first, then a bath.

Jenny stopped just before she pushed open the kitchen door. Yellow light splashed the floor beneath its wood. She could have sworn when she went to bed, she had turned off all the lights. Moving cautiously, she opened the door.

Sam was sitting at the kitchen table, his chair precariously tilted back. Music was hammering through his ear buds.

He tilted back another inch.

'Sam!' she cried.

He either didn't hear her or was deliberately ignoring her, for he didn't look around or acknowledge her presence. Jenny's cat, however, leaped off Sam's lap and streaked like a grey ghost toward her ankles.

She ran her hand along Twister's back, ending with a caress along his corkscrew tail. Then, with a sigh, she moved toward her son.

She touched his shoulder.

He shrugged off her hand.

She pushed back the hurt and tried not to react.

Sam had changed.

Puberty, Jake had said, when she

confided in him that her son had become an alien overnight.

When would it be over? she had demanded in response.

Hopefully Jake was right and Sam's problem was puberty. He was almost the right age. Twelve-years-old going on sixteen.

Sam's chair tipped further. Jenny caught and held it. Her son stared up at her, a question in his eyes.

'You're up early,' she said. 'Do you want some breakfast?'

'Had some,' he muttered.

She surveyed the table but saw no evidence of food or drink. 'What exactly did you have?'

In answer he turned and pulled the hood of his sweatshirt over his head. Then he turned up the volume of his music.

He might think he was all grown up, but the fingers sweeping across his iPod screen were still her little boy's, still pencil thin and childlike, not manly and strong. She longed to sweep her son into her arms.

Something he hadn't allowed in weeks.

She swallowed past the knot forming in her throat and pulled out his ear buds. 'I'll make us some scrambled eggs,' she offered.

'I don't want any,' Sam replied. But his hood slipped back and he watched as she pulled the egg carton from the fridge.

'There'll be no time for lunch,' Jenny hurried on. 'The wedding's at two.'

Sam scowled. 'I'm not going.' He lifted one foot and propped it on the table, an action he knew would drive her insane.

She caught her breath and counted to ten, then when that didn't work, went on to twenty. She could not allow Sam to get to her today, to make her worry or wonder if he was happy. Her best friend was getting married. Sam's best friend too. They would both do well to concentrate on that.

'Jake wants you at his wedding,' she

reminded her son softly.

Sam's scowl deepened.

'You know he's asked you to direct the guests down the path from the Country Club reception room to where the ceremony's taking place.'

'Someone else can do that.'

'Jake wants you.' Heaven only knew why. Months ago, when Jake had asked, she'd been delighted at the idea of her son taking part in her friend's special day. Now all she felt was fear and trepidation that Sam would do something to ruin the event. 'You promised,' she added.

'I'm hanging out with Mark.'

'Not today.' Jenny sat down next to Sam at the table.

'Jake won't notice if I'm not there.'

'He'll notice. So will I.'

Sam shrugged, turned away.

Jenny caught his chin and gently pulled him back to face her. 'We owe Jake, Sam. He's been good to us.'

'He doesn't need to bother.'

With a sigh, she drew her finger

along Sam's cheek, was pleased when he didn't flinch away. 'Jake doesn't consider it a bother, Sam.'

'Then why hasn't he come around here lately?'

'He's been busy. He's got a fiancée now. He has to spend time with her.'

Sam's entire body seemed to stiffen, and his fingers curled into his palm.

Worry surged through her. 'What is it, Sam?'

He didn't answer.

'You've been crabby all week,' she went on wearily.

A line formed between his eyes, and the gaze he turned on her was accusing. 'How come *I* was in your wedding pictures?'

Jenny's heart sank. Sam had looked at the wedding album a million times over the years, but had never before asked this question. 'You're my son,' she said lightly. 'Where else would you be?'

'I shouldn't have been there. I shouldn't even have been born.' The line between his eyes grew steadily deeper. 'Tony Vinelli said,' he went on, quoting the biggest know-it-all Pritchard Middle School had ever produced, 'that if a baby's born before his parents marry, then that baby's a . . . a bastard.' Sam said the last word with his chin jutted out as though he knew he'd used it in the right context, and not as a swear that could raise a protest from her. 'Am I a bastard?'

'No,' Jenny said, reaching for his hand.

He pulled it away.

'Names are just labels to categorize things,' she mumbled, groping for the words that would make him understand that he was no less than other kids just because she had been single when he was born. 'Names don't make a thing better or worse.' She had hoped he'd be older before asking about this, but had never been sure just how she would answer.

Her son's face now had the look of a bulldog. 'Why didn't Dad marry you before I was born?'

Her heart began to pound at double its speed and she could feel the perspiration on her brow. 'Is this what you've been worrying about?'

He nodded and his eyes were suddenly over-bright, as though he might cry and was fighting the inclination.

Jenny took a deep breath. 'Phil wasn't your father.' Her husband had been four years older than her and certain about things when it came to her and Sam. Especially certain that marrying him would be good for her, and that he would take care of her son.

She'd been desperate enough to agree to the plan and had done her best to be a good wife. Two years later, Phil had died, stricken by the same heart defect that had killed his father. The following year, Phil's mother, too, had died, so now there were no members of her husband's family left.

'Who was my father then?'

She almost missed Sam's question,

he'd asked it so quietly, but before she could answer, he added, 'It must be Jake.'

Jenny's breath left her lungs.

He glowered at her again. 'So why isn't Jake marrying *you*?'

'Jake isn't in love with *me*.'

'He should be. You could have made him.'

Jenny tried to grip hold of her swiftly fleeing patience. 'You don't *make* people fall in love.'

'You could have if you wanted to.'

'Honey — ' She touched his arm, was relieved when he didn't pull it away this time. ' — I'm not in love with Jake.'

'That's not what you said before.'

She frowned. 'What do you mean?'

'You're always telling me you love him.'

'As a friend, Sam!' A friend without whom they would both have been lost.

'Then why — ' Sam pressed his lips tight.

'Why what?'

11

'Why did you let him — ' Again her son stopped.

'Let him what?'

'Make a baby with you.'

'Jake's not your father.' It hadn't been Jake. It had never been Jake. She stood and grabbed a tea towel off its hook, then dabbed the moisture beading her forehead. She wished it was as easy to rub away the images lodged in her brain of Jake's best friend Matt Chambers.

She could still see Matt's face, could see his deep dark eyes and the lines bracketing his lips when he smiled. She remembered his heat forcing fire through her veins as they lay together against the back seat of his car.

'Jenny,' he had groaned, his lips hard against hers, tickling and driving her need to the surface.

'Matt,' she'd breathed back, loving his name, reveling in how it sounded on her lips. Matt and Jenny, she'd thought dazedly, linking their names in the way of all lovers.

12

Then, in an instant, all thinking was gone, lost in a wave of passionate kisses. She hadn't wanted him to stop, hadn't wanted him to know she'd never made love to anyone before. For suddenly she knew that's what they would do, in Matt's car, on that hill, in the wide back seat.

Jenny pressed the towel again to her face and cursed Matt Chambers to hell and back. Until that day thirteen years before, she'd never imagined making love could feel so good. Her parents had drummed fear of sex into her head, had warned her that boys couldn't be allowed to take advantage. Having sex brought trouble, loss of reputation, and worst of all, she might have a baby.

Having Sam had been a gift.

'Jake has to be my father,' Sam insisted, pulling Jenny back from memories that still burned.

'Why does he have to be?' Jenny asked.

'If it wasn't Dad, then it has to be Jake.' Sam spoke the words as though

13

he was desperate to know he had a father who was still alive, and one whom he liked almost as much as her. 'You've known him forever,' Sam added as though that fact clinched it.

'You're right, Sam, I have. And that's probably why he's just a friend. A best friend, one that I love, but just as a friend. He lived next door when I was growing up. You know that. You've seen my baby book. Birthday parties, Halloween . . . Jake was always there. He's like a brother to me.'

What Sam hadn't seen was how Jake had stood by her when Matt left for college back east. Leaving Jenny with a baby in her belly. Jake had encouraged her to finish high school, which she had done from home, course by course. When she graduated she had taken more courses to become a legal secretary so she could work for Jake at his law office.

'If Jake's not my father,' her son demanded hoarsely, 'tell me who is.'

Jenny glanced toward the counter

where Sam's puffer lay. He hadn't used it in a while. Hadn't had an attack. But the doctor had said to avoid stress, had said that in children stress often brought on asthma.

'This isn't the time to talk about this, Sam. We're due at Jake's wedding in less than two hours.'

'I have a right to know.'

'I agree. You do.' Jenny swallowed hard. 'But we can't talk about it now. Let's leave it until after Jake's wedding.'

'You promise?'

'I promise.' Although she didn't know how she could begin to tell him that his father had denied him since before he was born.

For an instant Sam looked as though he meant to throw up resistance, but in the end he slouched lower into his chair, pressed his lips tight, and closed his eyes.

2

When had the road to the Fair Winds Country Club become four lanes? Matt Chambers wondered as his cab sped past another car. And how in the hell had the grass got so green? Or had he simply forgotten how fresh the west coast vegetation was and how clear the air? At least, when it wasn't raining.

It had been ten years since he'd last been here and if Jake hadn't phoned asking him to be his best man, he wouldn't be here now.

He hadn't told his mother Jake was getting married, but that hadn't stopped her from finding out. She still read the *Seattle Times* cover to cover, and had spotted Jake's wedding announcement there. She might no longer live in their old home town, but his mother was up to date on who had been born, who had died, and who was

16

getting married.

Matt glanced at his watch and frowned. 'Hey, pal,' he called out to the driver, 'you need to step on it.'

'I'm already doing the speed limit, buddy.'

'Twenty bucks says the speed limit is higher.'

The cabby nodded and put his foot to the pedal.

'Over there,' Matt directed, when finally they maneuvered the last bend in the road.

The car was crawling now as it turned off onto the country club's driveway, joining a line-up of other guests. With a wave of his hand, Matt directed the cabby toward the side of the building. He'd told Jake he would meet him at the staff entrance, just as they had done when they were both fifteen and Matt was working his very first job. Back then he had arrived every Saturday morning before six, had washed the members' shoes and set out their clubs, then had hiked around the

17

course caddying for the pro.

It had been a different life back then, simpler, too, until Jenny had come along and flipped his world upside down.

Matt scowled at the intrusion of Jenny in his thoughts and slapped three twenties into the cabby's waiting hand. He brushed off the man's offer to carry his bag. His knee might be toast from too many tackles, but that didn't mean he needed help.

He heaved his bag out of the trunk and made his way up the gravel walkway, struggling as he went to dismiss images of Jenny, of her shape, her touch, and the welcome in her eyes.

Turned out that welcome had belonged to someone else, and the baby she carried had been someone else's too.

How could she have lied?

Especially after all they had promised each other.

Matt's jaw line tightened. It was long past time to douse the torch he'd been carrying for a woman who hadn't loved him as he loved her. He just hoped to God she wasn't at Jake's wedding, for he didn't want to see her without any warning. The thought of casting eyes on the girl he'd once loved felt tougher by far than facing any football linebacker. She had felled him before. He couldn't afford to let it happen again.

* * *

Jenny wasn't sure she could make it through the day, could watch Jake and Melissa's wedding with the attention it deserved and at the same time keep Sam out of trouble. The pain drumming her temples shot through to her skull.

If only she was able to confide in Jake, could tell him how out of hand Sam was getting. But she didn't want even Jake, her best friend and boss, to know she was failing as a parent.

Now Sam had disappeared. At the

country club's front door, he had cast one disdainful glance at the crowd in the foyer then slouched off in the direction of the country club's games room.

Which was probably just as well. He hadn't spoken one word on the long drive over, had only grunted when she reviewed his usher's task for the day. Jenny sighed and wished again she had said no when Jake had asked for Sam's assistance.

'Jenny! There you are. Where have you been?'

Jenny glanced up and saw her friend Vivian hurrying towards her, a glass of white wine in either hand.

'Take one,' Vivian ordered.

Jenny did so gratefully, then glanced at her watch. 'Do we have time?'

'A few minutes.'

'Cheers, then,' Jenny replied, clinking her glass against her friend's.

Vivian took a long sip. 'You're going to need that drink when I tell you who I just saw.'

'Who?'

Viv's lips twisted downwards. 'Amanda Perkins.'

'Amanda!' Jenny exclaimed. 'How is that possible? Her name wasn't on the guest list, and I should know. I typed it up myself.'

'She probably came as somebody's guest. Amanda always shows up at the best parties in town. You know that, girlfriend. And she always manages to make off with the hottest guy.'

Jenny smiled. 'Good thing it's a wedding. The cutest guy's taken.'

'There are plenty of cute guys.' Vivian's blue gaze swept the room. 'But I'm darned if I'm going to let Amanda snag them all.'

'May I remind you, girlfriend, that you're married to John?'

'I might be married, but you aren't.'

'And I don't want to be.' The protest came automatically, one of the many pronouncements she made regularly to her friend, if only to keep Vivian from organizing her life.

'Phil's been dead for years,' Vivian countered.

'I know. It's not that.' The two years she'd been married now seemed lost in time. She had cared for Phil, had loved him in a way, but he had barely left a mark on her life, not when compared to the passion she had felt for Matt.

'Then it's Sam,' Vivian said. 'You can't hide behind your son forever, Jenny.'

'I'm not hiding,' Jenny protested, silently cursing her friend's ability to zoom in on her hidden weakness.

'You've got to get a move on,' Vivian chided. 'Amanda's just split up with husband number two and she's ready to get her claws into husband number three.' Vivian leaned closer. 'We've got to make sure you get there first.'

'It's a whole new century. A woman doesn't need a man to make her happy.' Jenny took a sip of her Chardonnay. 'I'm a busy woman. I don't need a companion.'

'I was thinking more a lover.'

'Or a lover!'

'Every woman needs a yin to her yang. Besides,' Vivian added, 'how do you think it looks for my best friend to be dateless?'

'For me? Or for you?'

'For me, of course.'

'Get over it,' Jenny said.

Vivian gestured with her glass toward a stocky black-haired man. 'What about him?'

'That's Jake's cousin from Tacoma,' Jenny said, horrified. 'He's married and has three kids.'

'Or him,' Vivian went on, pointing this time to a tall, skinny man with a shock of red hair.

'I'll tell John,' Jenny threatened.

'This was John's idea.'

'It was not!' Jenny protested. 'Matchmaking is the last thing your husband would ever do.'

'He just wants to spread the joy of a committed partnership. He told me last night he's never been so happy.'

'Don't even think of telling me what

23

you were doing!'

'A little something involving whipped cream and chocolate.' Vivian licked a drop of liquid off her lip.

Jenny grimaced and took a larger sip of her wine.

'And then John said,' Vivian continued, 'that you might like to meet his friend Ted.'

'I wouldn't,' Jenny said firmly. She had met a friend of John's before and she had no intention of repeating the experiment. John's reputation for horrible taste was legion. The only thing he'd got right was choosing Vivian, and that was more because Vivian chose him.

'That's what I told him,' Vivian said with satisfaction. 'No woman in their right mind would want to date Ted. He's a workaholic and he watches sports on TV.'

Jenny chuckled.

Vivian smiled smugly. 'I told John *I* would find you a man.'

Jenny's amusement died. 'Sam — '

'Won't be with you forever.'

'Maybe not.' Jenny shifted to let a waiter slip between her and Vivian, placing her glass on his tray as she did so. 'But Sam needs me now. He's growing up so fast. I have to enjoy him while it lasts.'

Vivian scoffed. 'He's still a little boy.'

'A few more years and he'll be graduating from high school.'

Vivian's eyes took on a determined glint. 'All the more reason for you to meet a man.'

Jenny shook her head.

'It's your duty to provide Sam with a father.'

A week ago she would have teased Vivian back, would have said something flippant, something smart, but now what she felt was something like panic.

Vivian frowned. 'I thought you were sick of staying home on Friday nights watching action flicks on TV.'

'I like action flicks.'

'I know you do, girlfriend, especially when you watch them with Sam. But didn't you tell me the other day that Sam's out more and more; playing baseball, having sleep-overs — '

'Sometimes,' Jenny admitted, cutting her friend short, 'but often Sam's friends are over at our house.'

Vivian shuddered. 'I don't know how you do it. Sam's a darling, Jenny. You know I love him. But he *is* a boy. And when there's a whole herd of boys — '

'There's nothing wrong with boys.'

'They're smelly, they're always hungry and they make disgusting sounds.'

Jenny laughed. 'Only when they run in packs.'

'My point exactly,' Vivian said solemnly.

'They're also a lot of fun.'

'You didn't think that last Saturday when you had to fix Sam's bike.'

'So much grease,' Jenny agreed. Her hands had been black with it in the end. She had tried to change the chain, but had given up in despair, offering instead to help Sam with his math. He had told her long division wouldn't get him to his baseball practice, to which she had immediately offered to drive him. Too bad solving all Sam's problems wasn't as simple.

★ ★ ★

Jenny's kid must be twelve, almost thirteen. Incredible to think so much time could have passed. Matt had seen her from a distance the one time he'd been back, and Jake had told him the baby was a boy. A boy was good. Easier than a girl. You didn't have to worry about a boy getting pregnant.

After all this time, Jenny must have changed too. She wouldn't be the sexy teenager he'd left behind, with the wide blue eyes and wavy blonde hair, and the legs that seemed to stretch on forever. When she wore her spiked heels, she'd come up to his chin. Gangly was how she had always described herself, not recognizing what a knock-out she truly was.

Matt pushed open the side door to the Country Club and found himself in the corridor outside the locker rooms. Everything looked the same, Matt decided, pleased. Then the door to the men's locker room opened and Jake stepped through it.

'Hey,' Matt said, grinning at the sight of his friend in a black tux. The last time he'd seen him in these surroundings, Jake had been wearing tan slacks, a collared shirt and spiked shoes.

'Matt!' Jake exclaimed. 'I was beginning to think you'd never get here.' He took a step forward and pounded Matt on his back.

'I came straight from the airport,' Matt replied.

'You should have been here last night. You missed my stag.'

'I should have been the one organizing it.'

'Thank God you weren't,' Jake said, with a grin, 'or I'd still be standing somewhere tied naked to some tree.'

Matt's own grin widened. 'Now that

would be a sight I wouldn't want to see.' He shook his head. 'I'm sorry I couldn't get here any sooner. Things have been insane.'

'I'm just grateful you could get here at all. I know with your schedule you couldn't commit, but when Allen Carstairs had to bail as my best man — '

'What happened?'

'Burst appendix.'

'Ouch.' Matt studied Jake's face. 'So what did you do last night? You don't look hung-over.'

'That's because I'm not. Without you here to lead me astray, I managed to keep things under control.'

'I take it you didn't have any fun at all?'

'I've had all the fun I'm going to have as a single guy. Now all I want is to get hitched to Mel.'

'She's really got you hooked.' Matt shifted his case to his other hand. 'But that's great, Jake,' he said seriously. 'Don't let her go. You might regret it if you do.'

'Don't worry, buddy. The only place Mel's going is into my arms.'

Matt had thought Jenny would end up in *his* arms, but that dream had died when she lied. He stepped past Jake into the locker room. Green metal lockers still lined the walls and a smooth oak bench ran down the middle. 'Nothing's changed in here either,' he said, with satisfaction.

'Seattle's a small city, Matt. Not like Miami. Not all of us are running in the big leagues.'

'There's something nice about keeping things simple.'

'Is that why we're meeting in a locker room? On my wedding day yet?'

'I just thought the pungent odor of sweaty socks would make you appreciate all that you're giving up.'

'Mel's not going to make me give up golf.'

'You'll have to mow the lawn, build a picket fence — '

'Make love to the sweetest lady in the country.'

Matt smiled again. It was good to be back, to be hanging out with his friend. Thank God he and Jake had settled their differences. They had parted in anger after graduation, for he hadn't wanted to tell Jake that Jenny had cheated. Despite what she had done, he still felt the need to protect her.

'So tell me the truth,' Jake went on, 'did you come in this way so you wouldn't get mobbed?'

'Partly,' Matt answered. He had wanted somewhere private to ask about Jenny, hadn't managed to find the words when Jake had phoned him.

His gut lurched. He could blame it on the Scotch he'd downed on the plane with nothing but pretzels to catch the booze, but in the corner of his heart he seldom lifted he knew it was Jenny who caused his discomfort.

He sucked in a breath. 'I wondered if Jenny would be here today.'

'She'll be here.'

'I see.' Matt pursed his lips. 'It'll be good to see her,' he said, trying to mean it.

Jake's eyes narrowed. 'You've never called her then, since that time you were back?'

'You told me I shouldn't.'

'It was for the best. She was married . . . was happy . . . was getting on with her life.'

Like he had tried to get on with his, even though he had missed Jenny every day since he left.

'What about you?' Jake asked. 'Who's the lady in your life now? The papers keep linking you with one babe or another.'

'You know the press.'

Jake grinned. 'They never lie.'

'Don't tell my mother that. She's on at me all the time to settle down. She's always trying to set me up with daughters of neighbors living in her condo.' Matt shook his head. 'I told her I would find my own wife.'

'I saw a picture in one of the sports

magazines of some model you've been dating.'

'Brandi,' Matt murmured.

'She was hanging on your arm like she was never going to let go.'

'We've gone our separate ways.' Brandi was not the sort of girl he could introduce to his mother as potential daughter-in-law material, and Brandi had no intention of settling down.

'She was hot.'

'She was, but we didn't talk much.'

Jake tugged at the bow tie around his neck. 'They say talking's overrated.'

'She did talk about shoes.'

Jake groaned.

Matt grinned. 'She was always asking me whether their color matched her dress. Apparently, I never gave her the right answer. Color blind, she said.'

Jake chuckled and slapped him again on the back. 'It's great to see you again, Matt. It's been too long.'

'Thirteen years since I moved to Florida.'

'Seems longer, but then you left in a

mighty hurry. We pretty much had to eat your going-away cake ourselves.'

'Things were crazy back then.' He hadn't wanted to say goodbye, let alone eat cake. All he wanted was to put distance between him and Jenny.

'More than crazy,' Jake agreed. 'It's not every day Kent High produces a bona fide football star. Florida State, the most valuable player in the NFL, how much better could you do?'

'Plenty of good players have come out of Kent High.'

'Maybe now since you set up that scholarship fund. But you were the first to get a full ride.'

Matt shrugged again. His full ride had enabled him to go to university, had helped him put his sisters through too.

'You probably wouldn't even recognize the school now,' Jake went on. 'They put part of the grant you gave them towards a new stadium, they buy the team new uniforms every second year, and they've put in a whirlpool.

34

Coach Ramsey brags that it's as good as anything they have in the pros.'

'I'll have to see Coach while I'm here.' Matt had phoned the old man before he left Miami, was still grateful to him for the scholarship he had won.

'So what now?' Jake asked. 'I heard you're planning to coach.'

'Maybe,' Matt said.

'In Seattle?' Jake probed.

'I haven't decided.' The Seahawks had made him a very good offer, but he couldn't imagine settling in the same town as Jenny, no matter how much he missed the laid-back feel of the west coast, and the way Seattle sprawled along the edge of the ocean.

'I might just volunteer to coach kids,' Matt went on. Do for them what Coach had done for him. 'I'm ready for a change.' He glanced down at his right leg.

Jake frowned. 'Bad luck about the knee.'

'I'll live.'

'How about your mom and sisters?

35

How are they doing?'

'Great,' Matt said, 'although if I don't sign with my mother's beloved Seahawks, she just might disown me.'

'It'll never happen. Your mom thinks the sun shines out of your backside.'

Matt grinned. 'Well, the new job's a toss-up. The Dolphins have offered me a coaching position also.'

'No matter what you decide, your mom won't be disappointed.'

She'd have been disappointed if he'd lost his university scholarship and the subsequent honor of being the NFL's number one draft pick.

'You got to go where you wanted,' Jake went on. 'You had your pick of schools.'

'Florida State worked out well.' He had chosen the school that offered the most money, for money was the one thing his family lacked. His mother had worked two low-paying jobs in order to keep a roof over their heads, but her income didn't stretch to university. Besides which, as an added bonus,

Miami was on the opposite side of the country from Jenny.

'You all right Matt? You've turned a little pale.'

'I'm fine.' Or he would be. 'About Jenny — '

Jake glanced at his watch. 'I can't talk about her now. My wedding's about to start. I can't have my bride beating me to the ninth tee.' Jake jerked his head toward the lockers. 'Stick your bag in one of those and meet me on the course.'

3

Jenny edged past the people between her and the door, giving Vivian the slip when her friend went for more drinks. She needed to get outside, had to find Jake and Sam, had to brush off all thoughts of the past and of Matt. It was difficult here in this place where he had worked.

She had been surprised when Jake agreed to his mother's suggestion that they hold the wedding here. She hadn't thought the Club fit with her friend's style. But Jake said his wedding would not be a typical society do. Not once they were outside on the cliff overlooking the sea.

Another place she had no desire to go. For it was one of the last places she had been alone with Matt. With a sigh, she slipped past Mr. Jackson, one of their firm's oldest clients. He probably wouldn't recognize her away from the office where she sat behind her desk organizing Jake's day. And thank heavens for that. Right now she had no time to talk to anyone.

She wanted only to concentrate on Jake and his wedding, and make sure everything went off as planned. Jake now needed her just as much as she had needed him, had wanted her there early to make sure he didn't run.

But Jenny knew the only direction her boss would run would be towards his bride, not away as Matt had done.

The sun was bright as she passed through the doorway. Immediately, she turned left toward the cliff. She could see Jake ahead, together with Sam, and was struck again by the difference in her son. A month ago, Sam would have run down the path, not slouch along as he was doing now, scuffing dirt over his only pair of dress shoes.

Why couldn't Sam stay as he had always been?

The path took a turn. Jenny caught

her breath. The spot where Jake wanted his ceremony performed was as incredible now as when she'd last seen it. Only then it had been springtime, not early September, and Matt had been there to set her heart on fire.

'Jenny!'

With a start, she peered toward the cliff, covering her eyes against the sun. Jake and Sam were standing under the maple tree next to the ninth tee. The tree's enormous leaves were starting to turn. In a few more weeks, they'd be even more beautiful: orange and red, yellow and gold, green edged with brown.

Jenny moved towards them. 'Looking good, boss.'

'Back at you,' he said.

If Jake had turned he would have seen the spot where Matt had carved their initials in the tree, enclosing the letters with a large shaky heart.

Jenny glanced at her son standing next to Jake. 'Hey, Sam,' she said.

'Hey,' he muttered back.

40

Before she could say more, could give him a hug, he started back up the path toward the clubhouse.

'I'm not sure using Sam as an usher is a good idea,' Jenny said, frowning.

'He'll do fine,' Jake reassured her. 'People are like lemmings. Once the exodus begins, they'll all follow Sam here. Besides — ' He smiled. ' — my mother will make sure no one straggles. I only hope she doesn't get the bride to the altar too early!'

'Your mother seems so pleased.'

'She's just happy I'm getting married. She had almost given up hope. I have you to thank for that. If it hadn't been for you it might never have happened. I might not have paid attention when I met Mel.'

Jenny chuckled. 'You'd have paid attention all right. But whether you'd have taken the time to get to know Mel is another question.'

'That period of my life is over.'

'What? Making love first and asking questions later?'

'Or not asking them at all. It seemed such a waste of time. So many women, so few nights.'

'And now?'

'Just one woman, and still too few nights.' Jake smiled down at Jenny. 'I can't believe I met the woman of my dreams.' His blue eyes narrowed. 'Now we'll have to concentrate on you.'

'What do you mean?'

'Don't you think it's time to get back out there?'

'By *out there*, you mean dating, clubbing, and the like?'

'Why not? It'll be fun.'

'Not so much.'

'There's nothing holding you back. You should take a month off. Go someplace warm. Make love in the sun.'

'And Sam?' Jenny asked. 'What should I do with him while I'm off making love?'

'Leave him with Mel and me.'

'Right!' Jenny laughed. 'That's exactly what every bride wants after her honeymoon, a twelve-year-old boy to feed and get to school.'

'Mel would love it,' Jake said firmly. 'And so would I.'

Jenny shook her head. 'How about you concentrate on getting married before we start talking about babysitting for me.'

'I just want you to know I plan to hook you up with someone fabulous.'

Jenny groaned. 'I'll hold you to that, but what's with everyone today? Weddings should be about the bride and the groom, not the perfect occasion to set me up.'

'Who else has been trying?'

'Vivian.' Jenny winced. 'And you know what she's like.'

Jake grinned. 'Serves you right. You've meddled in our affairs often enough.'

'You needed help. So did Vivian.'

'Well, you haven't managed much in the love department lately!' The sun slanted off the ocean and struck Jake's eyes. 'And it's love you want, Jenny. Don't settle for less.'

She had settled for less when she married Phil. She had no intention of doing *that* again. But love? She didn't think so. All she knew about love is that it hurt too much.

* * *

So far Sam hadn't messed anything up. A few more minutes and the ceremony would begin. Her son's job would be over and she could relax.

The guests had surged obediently down the path and now waited, hushed, as the bride approached. This wedding was already doing what weddings did, reducing its viewers to a state of tears.

Jenny's eyes misted at the sight of Melissa walking over the grass on her father's arm, her hair a halo of bright curls and softness and her gaze fixed steadily on her husband-to-be. Jake, when Jenny glanced in his direction, was similarly entranced with his bride. There was a lifetime of welcomes in his smile.

Jenny smiled too. It had actually happened. Her friend had fallen in love, and had made it to the altar. She touched Sam's shoulder as he moved to stand beside her, but, his lips set mutinously, he shrugged her hand away.

She pressed her fingers to her brow and tried to eradicate the line she knew was forming between her eyes. Her mother had chastised her the last time she came to visit, had said frowning created dents that would deepen as she aged.

With a sigh, Jenny also willed her facial muscles to relax, and then pushed back her hair and focused on the bridal couple. They stood side by side facing the minister, and behind the minister was the late summer sky. Below the sky, the ocean swelled.

Although there were inches between Jake and Melissa, the love they shared wrapped tangibly around them. They were beautiful, romantic, the perfect couple. The sort of couple Jenny had always wanted to be part of.

Impossible to attain with a twelve-year-old child. What worked for two didn't work for three. And Sam came first. Always had, always would.

The minister intoned the words, 'In sickness and in health, until death do you part.'

Longer than most people cared to commit. Then Jake and Mel turned and she knew that *they* had. They faced each other, their eyes alight, and their lips turned up in love-warmed smiles.

Tears pricked Jenny's eyes. If things had been different, this could have been her. Not here, not now, but before and for always. She could have been staring into her lover's eyes and seen his love staring back at her.

She averted her gaze from Jake and his bride and in that instant her world swept away.

Eyes of blue slate stared into hers from the face of the tall man to the right of the groom. He was standing in the spot Allen Carstairs should be

46

standing. She would have registered that Allen wasn't there if she hadn't been daydreaming of times long past.

Instinctively, she clenched her fingers, felt her nails bite into her son's shoulder.

The new best man stood as though bracing for a storm, with his legs apart and his eyes like thunder. Jenny drew Sam close, and stepped in front, determined to shield him from Matt Chambers' gaze.

How could Matt be here? He hadn't been invited. And according to an item she'd heard on the news, he was supposed to be three thousand miles away, training the new rookies at Florida State to sweat and grunt their way down a football field.

But then Matt Chambers never played by the rules.

He'd broken her heart and moved away, had left her with a baby in her belly. A baby that was now too big to be hidden. A baby almost the size of her.

Sweat beaded her forehead. She had

47

to get Sam away before Matt saw him. But before she could move, Matt's gaze shifted. He stared at Sam, his brows forming a straight line above his nose.

She had often told Sam they were two against the world, but it would be easier to fight the world than it would be to fight Matt.

She bent towards her boy and whispered in his ear, 'Hustle back to the clubhouse, sweetie. There's something else you have to do.'

Sam frowned. 'Jake said my job was done when the ceremony was over.'

'Just do as I say, for goodness sake.' The reluctance in his eyes told her it would take a rocket beneath his feet to make him go anywhere else.

'What am I supposed to be doing?'

'Go out to our car and open the trunk. There's a box of tin cans inside.'

'Ah, Mom,' he moaned. 'We can't recycle now.'

'There's string tied to the cans. Get them out and tie the cans to Jake's car.'

Sam's expression cleared. 'What

about a '*Just Married*' sign? Did you make one of those?'

'I did,' Jenny said. 'It's in the box too.'

'Cool,' Sam said, a smile lighting his face.

She wanted to hug him, to tell him she loved him, to hold him and protect him from all that threatened. But she took a deep breath, and simply smiled back, giving him the thumbs up as he ran.

People swarmed to greet the bride and groom, but Jenny's gaze shifted back to Matt. She squared her shoulders. She wasn't going to run.

Matt turned and held out his hand to Jake. 'Congrats!' he said. 'You actually did it.'

Jenny couldn't believe it. She had assumed that if ever the two met again, she would see Jake attempt to punch Matt out. But instead Matt was here as Jake's best man, and the two were talking, no tension in their stances. Then, as she watched, Matt gave Jake a hug.

She remembered how it felt to be in Matt's arms, remembered his warmth and the smell of his cologne. Once there she had never wanted to be any place else.

But why was Jake acting so friendly? And why, for heaven's sake, was Matt the best man? As far as she knew they hadn't seen each other in years, had never spoken since Matt went away.

So what was this?

Some weird sort of male bonding?

Or had Jake forgotten what Matt had done?

Jenny's heart began to thump, and it was beginning to feel as though she'd never breathe again. Then suddenly Jake turned and brought Melissa forward, and holding her hand, introduced her to Matt.

Jenny turned away, willing her legs to move, but her body betrayed her as thoroughly as Jake. She couldn't seem to shift from her spot, and then a hand clamped her shoulder and spun her around.

4

'I wasn't sure when I came if you'd be here,' Matt said.

She stared into his eyes and tried to ignore the current flowing between them. 'Where else would I be? It's not me who took off.'

'I thought seeing you would be easier.'

'Nothing between us has ever been easy.'

'It used to seem as though it was,' he said gruffly.

Making love had been easy. Losing him had been hard. She had thought she had found her partner for life, had thought they had between them a magic that would last forever.

Now she couldn't bear to gaze into his eyes, didn't want to see again that the magic was gone. Was equally afraid to find out it wasn't.

'This was our old spot,' he said, glancing toward the tree.

So he'd remembered too.

'Remember the golfer,' Matt said, his voice low.

Jenny's face grew hot. She had thought on that night that they'd finally make love, in this spot with the sound of the sea crashing below. But the golfer had come upon them while they were locked in an embrace, making enough noise to spring her and Matt apart.

'So how have you been?' Matt asked, moving on, as though she were some acquaintance to whom he was making small talk.

'Why ask? You don't care.'

'Your son, then?' he demanded.

She looked into his eyes, saw the blackness then the light. 'What son?' she asked, lifting her chin.

'The boy who was standing beside you earlier. The one who looks just like you.'

Relief poured over Jenny like a cool breeze on a hot day. Matt hadn't realized with his usual sixth sense that the boy he had seen was also *his* son. Then as swiftly as it had come, the relief segued into rage. How could Matt not know? She had told him after all. And now that he had seen Sam, how could he not see that her boy was his? Did he intend once again to deny his own blood?

Matt stepped closer. 'I didn't believe he was mine.'

She took a step back. 'I told you he was.'

'I believe you now.'

She had thought she wanted to finally hear him say those words, even if it had taken him thirteen years to do so, but all she felt at this moment was sheer and utter terror.

'His eyes,' Matt went on. 'My grandfather had eyes like your boy's.'

Like Matt's eyes also, Jenny suddenly realized, as she stared directly into them. She had tried not to acknowledge that resemblance before, hadn't wanted to connect her son to the man who had broken her heart.

She lowered her gaze, then immediately regretted it, for lower was Matt's mouth and the lips she'd once kissed. She took another step away. The tension between them did not disappear. 'Go away,' she said.

'I'm not going anywhere.'

'I don't want you here.'

'So,' Matt went on, as though she hadn't spoken, 'you were telling the truth.'

Jenny couldn't speak, her throat was so dry.

'I thought you were lying.'

'Your problem, not mine.' Matt not believing had hurt so much. She had always believed every word he uttered. 'I trusted you.'

His eyes grew darker. 'I trusted you too. I thought you had betrayed that trust.' He glanced toward the Club House to where Sam had disappeared. 'Now I've missed so much time, so many years. Why didn't you call? You could have called.'

'And told you what? I had already told you face to face that I was pregnant. You didn't believe me then. Nothing had changed.'

'We could have talked when things were calmer.'

'When do you imagine things got calmer? When my belly had grown to the size of a basketball? Or when I was on my way to the hospital?'

'After the baby was born. When you could see . . . could know that the baby was mine.'

'I knew that from the beginning. It was only you who didn't believe.'

Matt lifted his hand and ran his fingers through his hair, messing it up in the way she remembered. 'You don't even look as though you carried a child, Jenny. You're very slim.'

'Not like before.' Since carrying Sam, she had curved more around her hips, and her breasts were fuller than they'd been as a teen.

He shook his head. 'Girls never think they're thin enough. They're always dieting. God knows why.'

'To please guys. We're fools.'

'You never dieted.' His gaze roamed her body, lingered on her breasts.

She cursed her nipples, now pressing hard against her dress despite her best efforts to convince herself that she no longer desired this man she'd once loved. 'No willpower,' she said curtly. 'But I did diet once.'

'I don't remember.'

'It was when I first thought I might be pregnant.'

He frowned, said nothing.

'I was really afraid. I hoped that maybe if I didn't gain weight, it wouldn't be true that I had a baby inside.' She touched her stomach, remembering that time. 'It didn't work.'

He reached out his hand and placed it on hers.

'Don't touch me,' she ordered.

He couldn't force his hand away. Her skin was just as he remembered; warm, smooth and silky beneath his fingers.

Her eyes widened as though she was

remembering too, how he had touched, had explored her body's curves. As a young woman, she had looked amazing. She looked even more amazing now.

But he had left, hadn't believed what she said. It was no surprise she didn't trust him now. He glanced around and saw that all the guests had gone, were already back up at the Club House.

Jenny's gaze followed his. 'I've got to go.'

'We have to talk.'

'We have nothing to say.'

There were so many words swirling in his brain, he had difficulty forming them into a single sentence. 'We have to talk about our child,' he finally said.

'I'm not talking about Sam. Not with you.' She gulped in a breath, as though she regretted saying the boy's name aloud.

'I want to meet him,' he said firmly.

A red spot glistened on each of Jenny's cheeks. 'You can't come back after all these years and start telling me what you want.'

'That's not what I'm doing.' He forced his voice even. 'We've got a problem. We need to solve it.'

'We had a problem thirteen years ago. We have nothing now.'

'Jenny!' He stopped and sucked back his frustration, tried to regain calm before speaking again. 'I want to meet the boy.'

Jenny's eyes grew stormy. 'You say he's your son then you call him *the boy*!'

He didn't know what else to call him. Saying *son* seemed unreal, and calling him by his name seemed far too intimate while his brain still reeled from the fact Sam was his. 'Sam,' he said aloud, experimenting with the word. It fit on his tongue, seemed to linger in the air.

'I don't care what you call him, boy or Sam,' Jenny snapped. 'You're not going to meet him.' The color on her cheeks had now disappeared and in its place was an icy paleness.

Matt was sure his face looked the

same, for all heat had left, leaving him frozen. 'You can't stop me Jenny.'

'I can. I will.' She sounded as desperate as she looked. 'It's Jake's wedding day. Don't spoil it for him.'

'Me meeting my son won't spoil anyone's day.'

Jenny straightened her shoulders. 'So what do you think's going to happen? That I'll simply let you walk up and introduce yourself?'

'The Jenny I remember would want me to know him.'

'Not now. Not like this,' she said, in a steely voice.

'Does he know I'm his father?'

'No.'

Pain stabbed Matt's temples. 'When were you planning on telling him that?'

'Never, I hoped.' She pressed her lips together.

'So you intended he never know who his real father was?'

'Maybe,' she said, but her eyes flickered sideways. 'I thought I might tell him when he was older.'

59

'How old?' he demanded.

'I don't know,' she replied. 'When and if I felt the time was right.'

He ignored the warning in her eyes. 'The time is right now.'

'It's not up to you what I say and when.'

'I'm here now, Jenny. I want to meet Sam.'

'You're twelve years too late.'

'I'm not going away.'

Was this the way she'd had to fight, like a tigress defending her cub from all comers? While he was off playing games for a living, she had cared for the child they'd created together.

'Jenny,' he said, more gently this time. He didn't want to scare her or cause her distress. If he could he would now do everything differently. He wouldn't listen to Coach or anyone else, would find an explanation for what he'd seen with his own eyes. He reached out his hand and covered hers with it.

Jenny flinched away.

Matt moved forward, crowding into her space. 'What about your husband?' he demanded. 'Does Sam think he's his father?'

'I don't have a husband. Not anymore.' And as of this morning, Sam no longer thought Phil was his Dad.

'What happened?' Matt asked.

'Phil died,' she replied.

'I'm sorry,' he said.

Jenny glanced toward the ocean. The waves were crashing harder than before. They seemed to match the turmoil in her heart. She lifted her chin and turned back to Matt. 'How did you even know I was married?'

'Jake told me.'

'When?'

'When I came back to Seattle after finishing my degree.'

'You came back?' Her voice caught. 'I didn't see you.' She would have been married a whole year by then. Sam would have been four.

'I wasn't here long. I caught the red eye from Miami, flew in, had breakfast with Jake, then flew out again.'

'Why did you come?'

'Why do you think?' His eyes were so black she could lose herself in them. 'I came to see you.'

Before her wedding she had wondered what Matt would do if he knew she was about to be married. In her dreams he had always come back to stop it. Foolish dreams. Naive.

'Jake told me then that you were married,' Matt went on. 'He also said you were happy.'

Moisture welled in Jenny's eyes. *Matt* had made her happy until he accused her of betrayal.

'I hoped we could put things right,' Matt said, 'could somehow get past everything that had gone wrong.'

Jenny shut her eyes, heard again the pain that had been in his voice that time long ago when he had accused her of lying. Swiftly, she opened her eyes again.

Matt drew closer, as though he was going to touch her again. 'Jake said you were settled in your new life. He said seeing you would serve no purpose.'

'So you just went home?'

'No.' He touched her hand. 'I couldn't go.'

She couldn't pull away.

'I drove to your house. I had to see for myself.'

'I didn't see you.'

'I saw you. And Phil,' he added. 'The guy you once told me wasn't your boyfriend.'

Her body grew stiff.

Matt cleared his throat. 'I parked on your street, saw you get out of a blue station wagon. A little boy was in the back. You got him out and took his hand. Phil came around the car and took his other hand. You swung him between you as you walked up the sidewalk.'

'Sam always thought he was flying when we did that.'

'You looked happy,' Matt said.

'So you left?' Jenny whispered.

'What else could I do?'

Matt obviously thought letting things lie had been a gift. She wasn't so sure.

'So what about Sam?' Matt asked her now. 'Who does he think his father is?'

'He doesn't know.'

'Surely he's asked?'

'No,' she lied. 'He hasn't given it a thought.'

His dark gaze narrowed.

'It's like Jake said. He's happy, Matt. Don't mess that up.'

'I don't intend to mess anything up, but I can't just leave things. Not now that I know.'

She tried to move around him, to escape back to the clubhouse where the other guests were. 'You had your chance.'

'I made a mistake.'

'I thought you loved me.' She strained to make her voice audible. 'I know I loved you. That should have been enough.'

'Love isn't everything.'

It had been for her. When Matt turned his back on her and their baby, something in her soul had died. 'I don't want you in my life,' she said, her voice coming out strangled.

'And Sam?' he demanded.

'Sam's happy without you.' She turned her head away, not wanting Matt to see she had bold-facedly lied.

5

Something hurt in her gut. She wasn't
sure what. It could be the fact she'd
eaten none of the wedding dinner, or
perhaps was the fault of the white wine
she had drunk. Her glass refilled like
magic every time it got empty, and if
Melissa didn't throw her bouquet soon,
Jenny just might throw up.

She needed to escape, to grab Sam
and go before Matt insisted they talk
again. She had tried to leave when she
fled the wedding scene, had run as fast
as she could in two-inch heels back to
the clubhouse, but for once, perversely,
Sam hadn't wanted to leave.

Which meant she had spent the last
two hours watching Sam out of one eye
and Matt from the other. It was giving
her a headache as well as a gut ache
and she was starting to see black spots
before her eyes.

'Hey, Jenny,' Vivian said, coming up beside her and clinking her glass against Jenny's own, 'have you seen Mr. Right yet?'

'No,' Jenny snapped, peering over her friend's shoulder, trying with all her might to keep Sam in her sights.

'What about that guy talking to Jake?'

Unable to stop herself Jenny glanced in Jake's direction, and saw, to her horror, that the man was Matt. 'No thanks,' she muttered, chugging back a gulp of wine.

'He's cute,' Vivian went on, rising to her toes to peer around Mike Pearson, who had played center forward on the senior boys' basketball team the year after Jake and Matt had graduated.

Jenny hadn't caught any of the games that year. She'd been far too busy taking care of her baby. But Jake had filled her in as only a man would, chatting about sports when uncertain what to say.

Matt hadn't ever had any difficulty conversing, even though football had been his life. When they were alone, he concentrated on her, never once uttering the dreaded word playoffs. Instead they talked about the places they would go after they had both graduated from college.

Jenny glowered in the direction of Matt's dark head. He had probably already gone to all the places on their list. But, her heart lightened, he didn't have Sam.

Sam made up for everything.

'He's looking over here.' Vivian dropped to her soles and faked nonchalance.

'Ignore him,' Jenny instructed.

'But you like the tall, dark and handsome type.'

'Handsome is as handsome does.' Jenny winced. Seeing Matt again was really stressing her out, for she was suddenly doing what she never did, quoting one of her grandmother's many old wives' sayings.

In this case it was true. Matt Chambers was handsome even if he hadn't behaved so, and she should be glad he had left as he did.

For he hadn't loved her. And if he didn't love her, she didn't want to love him. Unfortunately, you didn't always get what you wanted.

'Cute butt, too,' Vivian said approvingly. 'You know what a sucker you are for cute butts.'

'That's you,' Jenny replied, looking again to see where Sam had got to. It was beginning to feel like a game of cat and mouse, keeping track of her son and Matt at the same time.

'My God, look at his eyes.'

'If you keep staring at him, Vivian, he's going to come over.'

'That wouldn't be so bad,' her friend all but purred. 'I'll take him if you don't want him.'

'You're married, remember?'

'A guy like that could make a girl forget.'

'Just be glad you don't know what a guy like that can do.'

'Honey,' Vivian admonished, 'you

sound positively bitter.'

'Let's just say, I have my reasons.'

'Think how great it would be for Sam to have a dad.'

'Sam's done perfectly well without one so far.'

'That's not what you said when Sam needed a father for his Scout troop campout.'

'Your John didn't mind standing in as Sam's dad.'

'That's not the point. My John, bless him, doesn't know how to camp out, doesn't know one end of the axe from the other. Sam was lucky they came home alive. John probably paid some other dad to chop their wood. A real dad. A he-man.'

'Are you calling that guy a he-man?'

'Yes,' Vivian said, with an appreciative sigh. 'He's got muscles — '

'How can you tell?'

'By the way his jacket spreads across his shoulders.'

Jenny had run her hands over Matt's muscles, could still remember how they moved. Matt had whispered her touch made him weak, that she was Delilah and he was Samson. Matt's coach had actually told Matt to stop seeing her before games.

Not that Matt listened.

One thing at least she knew for sure; she would never tell Vivian that Matt was Sam's father. She'd only known Viv since working for Jake, but she had a best friend's proclivity for telling her what to do.

And Vivian's advice always sucked. Would involve, as usual, difficulties for herself. Vivian was an incurable romantic. She would definitely think Matt was the answer to Jenny's prayers, would say he had come home in the nick of time to save her and Sam from a life of eternal loneliness.

Vivian tugged on Jenny's arm. 'You have got to look at his eyes!'

'I'd just as soon not!' Matt's eyes had a way of making her want what she shouldn't have. Bedroom eyes, some would call them. Lover's eyes, she substituted, for they weren't bedroom eyes in the usual sense of the word. He didn't come on to each and every woman. What he did was choose so that the woman felt special, then he'd swiftly mesmerize that woman for life.

It had been life for her, if how her body still reacted was anything to go by. He made her feel, even when they were arguing, that she was the prettiest, sexiest woman around.

Vivian curled her tongue around the olive in her martini. 'I wouldn't mind ending up in his bed, that's all I'm saying.'

'Don't say it. Don't even think it. You know you don't mean it. What you and John have is something special.'

'I wouldn't mind occasionally shaking things up.'

Jenny groaned. 'Don't you dare! I still haven't got over the last time you shook things up.'

'How was I to know your mother would come over, that she'd read your e-mail?'

'I keep all my recipes on my computer. I've told you that a million times.'

'You didn't tell me your mother reads them!'

'My mother always does what I least expect.' At which thought Jenny glanced swiftly around the room in case her mother had come home early from visiting her cousin in Portland and showed up unexpectedly at Jake's wedding.

She had never told Lillian Holden the name of Sam's father for fear her mother would try to fix things. But if her mother met Matt, she wouldn't need to be told, for she had a highly developed intuition when it came to secrets. She'd be on to Matt like a heat-seeking missile causing God knows what harm to Sam in the process.

Jenny hadn't wanted anyone to hold a gun to Matt's head. If he didn't love her and want to be with her, she didn't want him at all.

'You have to admit,' Vivian went on,

73

dragging Jenny's focus back to her, 'that there were some interesting people in that chat room.'

'Kinky is the word you're searching for.'

'That guy with his secret sex position — '

'Secret sex position?' Matt enquired.

Jenny spun around, and found Matt so close their bodies almost touched.

'On Jenny's computer,' Vivian said confidingly.

'Vivian,' Jenny warned.

'Well, it was,' Vivian insisted. 'It was something involving handcuffs and a cucumber — '

'Enough,' Matt said, holding up his hands. He glanced at Jenny. 'I didn't know you went in for such things.'

Vivian stared at her accusingly. 'And you didn't tell me you knew this man.'

'I don't tell you everything, either of you!' Jenny's head had begun to spin again and her body felt as though it would soon follow suit.

'Aren't you afraid,' Matt asked, 'that

Sam will see which internet sites you go to?'

'It's not me — ' She shut her mouth. She did not have to explain anything, especially to Matt.

'Jenny was making a list,' Vivian said, 'of all the sites she wanted to block from her computer.' She shifted her drink from her right hand to her left then held out her right hand to take hold of Matt's. 'I'm Vivian,' she said, introducing herself.

'Matt Chambers,' Matt replied, with an answering smile.

'How do you know Jenny? She's never mentioned you.' Vivian bestowed on Jenny her best disapproving look.

'We're old friends,' Matt replied.

'More Jake's friend than mine,' Jenny added quickly. 'He was in Jake's class. Matt's two years older than me.'

'The older man,' Vivian murmured.

Matt's smile deepened. 'I'm not sure I want to be known as the older man.'

'I don't see why not,' Vivian went on.

75

'People say experience counts. What do you say, Jenny?'

'Depends on what you're experienced in.' Her throat grew tight. When she was sixteen, she didn't know about experience. She only knew making love to Matt felt good.

'Where's John?' Jenny asked, wanting to change the subject. She didn't want to think of making love or Matt Chambers.

'Somewhere,' her friend answered, her gaze still on Matt.

'John is Vivian's husband,' Jenny went on. 'They're celebrating their tenth anniversary this year.'

'Ten years. Wow!' Matt glanced at Jenny. 'A lot can happen in ten years.'

'It can,' she agreed, tension lodging in her chest.

Vivian sighed and drained the rest of her Martini. 'I'd better go and find John before he finds me. I promised I would be the designated driver this evening. If I know John, he'll be enjoying the free drink and food.' She held up her empty glass. 'I know I have.'

'Take my taxi,' Matt offered. 'I told the driver to wait. He can take you both home then come back for me.' He turned to Jenny. 'For you and your son, also, if you like.'

Thank God he hadn't referred to Sam as *his* son. Vivian would have caught on to *that* with the speed of light.

'I'll take you up on that.' Vivian smiled at Matt warmly. 'As long as you let me return the favor.'

Jenny stared at her friend in dismay, having been the unwelcome recipient of many a favor. *Just go home*, she silently begged.

But Vivian wasn't even looking at her. She was concentrating on Matt with the single-minded focus that had made her a shark in the advertising business. 'How about dinner tomorrow night?' she suggested. 'Me and John, you and Jenny. You can catch up on old times.'

'We don't have old times,' Jenny said in a threatening voice, but her friend was so far gone in her own fantasy world that she didn't hear, or chose not to, the fact that her invitation was unwelcome.

'Sounds great,' Matt agreed. He smiled at Vivian, a devastatingly broad smile.

Like butter wouldn't melt, Jenny thought.

'Bring Sam too,' Vivian added.

'Bring Sam where?' a treble voice asked, as Sam appeared behind Vivian and sidled into their threesome.

'My place,' Vivian replied. 'Dinner, kiddo. Steaks, hamburgers, the works.' She cupped her hand under Sam's chin. 'What do you say? We can rent a movie, too, or your favorite video game.'

'Great!' Sam said, then threw a questioning glance at Jenny.

She hated that Sam seemed to expect her to say no, but she definitely had to say no this time. She didn't want her son to spend the evening with Matt, a man who could blow their world apart.

'You've got that science project due, Sam.'

'I hate science,' Sam replied.

Matt stepped forward. 'I could help with that.'

'Who are you?' her son answered.

6

Jenny held her breath and prayed.

'My name's Matt Chambers.' He held out his hand.

Thank God he hadn't introduced himself as Sam's father.

'I've heard of you.' Sam's eyes grew wide. 'You play football for the Miami Dolphins.' He took hold of Matt's hand and shook it hard.

A fine time for her son's manners to kick in.

'I'm not playing for them now.' Matt glanced down at his leg.

His eyes had flickered swiftly, but Jenny could tell from the tightening of his jaw that the twisted knee she'd heard discussed on the news caused Matt pain beyond the merely physical.

'I've never met a football star before,' Sam said, his gaze glued to Matt as though he was a wish granted by some genie.

'You like football?' Matt asked.

'Who doesn't?' Sam answered.

'Do you play?'

'No, he doesn't.' Jenny tried to move between the two, but when she took a step, Sam stepped too.

'Aw, Mom, I do so,' Sam protested, almost tripping over her foot in his efforts to keep Matt in sight.

'Since when?' she asked, stunned.

'Every kid plays football,' Matt said, with a grin. Then he snatched a bread roll from a nearby table. 'Catch,' he said, tossing the roll to Sam.

Her son held out one hand and caught the roll neatly.

'A natural,' Matt said, slapping Sam on the back.

Jenny sucked in some air. Her son probably only played the odd pickup game, but with Sam's asthma any exertion could result in him struggling to force oxygen into his lungs. One more thing she didn't want Matt to know, for the more he knew, the more he'd want to know.

'How about you and I throw the ball around tomorrow?' Matt suggested.

'Yes!' Sam exclaimed. He turned to Jenny. 'How come you never told me you knew Mr. Chambers?'

'Matt, call me Matt.'

Sam shot Matt a grin, then turned back to Jenny with an accusing look.

'He's more a friend of Jake's,' she said, explaining.

'He graduated from the same high school as you, Mom.'

Technically, she hadn't actually graduated from Kent High. Her pregnancy had interfered with that. She'd taken correspondence courses to complete her eleventh and twelfth grades.

'I've seen his picture in the school's trophy case,' Sam went on, 'next to the trophy for the State Championship he won.'

'The team won, buddy,' Matt corrected.

'Without you, the team sucked.'

'Without the team, there is no game.'

The throbbing in Jenny's head revved into overdrive. Matt and Sam were talking as though this were normal, as though father and son weren't meeting for the first time.

'So why didn't you tell me?' Sam persisted.

'We haven't seen each other in a long time,' Jenny replied.

Vivian beamed. 'All the more reason for us all to get together then. What about tomorrow night?'

'No,' Jenny said swiftly. 'Sam has school the next day.'

'I'll make dinner early,' Vivian assured her.

'He's got homework,' Jenny added.

'Matt said he'd help me with my project,' Sam reminded her.

'And any other homework you have,' Matt offered. 'I'm pretty good at math.'

Jenny glared at Matt. How dare he push this when she had said no, and why in heavens wasn't her son protesting about doing homework? If she'd been the one to suggest it, he'd have trotted out every excuse under the sun.

'After we're done,' Matt went on, 'we'll throw around the football.'

'That's settled then,' Vivian said.

'Vivian,' Jenny said, from between clenched teeth, 'could you do me a favor?'

'Sure,' her friend replied. 'Just don't ask me to let you bring those chocolate Florentines for dessert. The last time you made those, I gained five pounds.'

'No Florentines,' Jenny agreed. She nodded toward her son. 'Could you and John take Sam with you and drop him home? I want to say goodnight to Jake and Melissa. It might take a few minutes.'

Vivian's gaze shifted to Matt then back to Jenny, then she took Sam by the hand. 'OK, handsome, let's find John.' She winked at Jenny. 'Take your time, girlfriend. We'll hang out with Sam until you get home.'

Jenny caught her breath, wanting to set her friend straight, but all the words that came to mind just sounded stupid. Which about summed up how she felt. It was a feeling she didn't like, and one she hadn't had since leaving high school.

With a sigh, she faced Matt. 'Thanks for not saying anything to Sam.'

'Not yet,' Matt replied.

'What do you mean?'

He took a step closer.

She felt suddenly overwhelmed by Matt's size and his scent, subtle yet powerful, enticing yet bold. She stepped backwards and found herself against a table. She gripped its hard edge and tried to steady the dizziness rocking her brain. It could have been the wine or the intoxicating rhythm of the band, but she knew without a doubt the dizziness was due to Matt.

'Sam seems like a great kid,' Matt said, ignoring her question.

She tried to speak, to demand an answer, but the faculty of speech had disappeared. Then a couple making their way onto the dance floor bumped against Matt and his body hit hers, discombobulating her even further.

She and Matt seemed to be the only ones not moving. But inside it was as if nothing stood still. Her blood shot through her veins at a tempest-filled pace, and her muscles flexed and shifted as though weighing up flight or fight.

She didn't want to fight, but she would if she had to, if that's what it took to keep her son safe.

If only Matt's lips weren't mere inches from her own. If only she didn't suddenly want to kiss him.

'You've done a great job,' his low voice went on.

She'd done it on her own. He hadn't helped.

'Sam's a credit to you.'

'You don't know him,' she said.

'I've seen enough to know that you've raised him well.'

She didn't want Matt's praise,

couldn't allow herself to care. She'd cared before and still he had left. But she couldn't stop the heat spreading across her cheeks, couldn't convince herself it was a normal mother's reaction to words of praise regarding her offspring. In her heart, she knew it was more than that. It was a reaction to the man himself.

She chewed her bottom lip. She had to get away, also had to get Matt to agree to leave town.

Then his gaze left hers and drifted lower, landing on her lips and lingering there. She opened her mouth to protest, but her words tangled in her tongue, which seemed swollen in her throat, and her heart was pounding too fast to breathe.

Then he reached towards her and put his hand on her waist and all thoughts of protest withered and died. The noise of the room and the people surrounding them dipped in volume to the lapping of waves.

She felt buffeted . . . pulled . . . like a

starfish in a tide. Matt's energy, presence, took over her own.

'Jenny,' he murmured, his free hand taking hers, pulling her closer until her breasts hit his chest.

She uttered a sound like a sigh gone hollow. 'Don't,' she whispered. She lifted her hand to push him away, but found herself trapped in decade-old desire.

'Let's dance,' Matt said softly. Without waiting for an answer, he took her in his arms.

She could barely stand, let alone dance. Whatever magic Matt had cast had removed all her bones. Yet when he whirled her onto the floor, she melted against him with the fluidity of water.

She didn't know if the music was fast or slow. She only knew that they danced cheek to cheek, hip to hip.

She remembered the times they had been alone, when she'd had the privacy and need to touch him. She didn't want to feel as she had before, but didn't know how to stop the desire.

His hand swept her back, revitalizing . . . thrilling her. She tried to pull away, to stop all response. She breathed in deeply, tried to find air. Then she pressed her hand against his chest, but felt her resistance sweeping away.

'May I cut in?' Jake asked, suddenly approaching from behind.

'Later,' Matt replied, not releasing his hold.

'Yes,' Jenny countered, grasping Jake's hand as though it were a lifeline. His fingers were cool compared to Matt's. Dancing with Jake wouldn't leave her legs weak.

'Mel and I are leaving soon,' Jake said simply. 'I want a dance with Jenny before I go.'

With a nod, Matt stepped away.

'How are you doing?' Her boss's gaze searched hers.

She tried to catch her breath. 'Not so good.'

'At least seeing Matt hasn't killed you.'

'Give it time. Why didn't you warn

me he was coming?'

'I didn't want you to run.' His hold on her waist tightened as though he still worried that she might.

'What's he doing here, Jake?'

'He's filling in as best man.'

'Jake,' she said warningly.

'He came to see you.'

She tried to stop her heart from pounding clear through her chest. 'Why now?' she demanded.

'It's time you two talked, maybe even tried to fix things.'

She turned her face away. 'Nothing's broken,' she said. 'Sam and I are doing just fine.'

'I know you are, which is why Matt being here won't hurt the two of you.'

She wished she could tell Jake how vulnerable she felt, how difficult Sam had been in the last little while. She pulled in a shaky breath. 'I hope you're right.'

'People change,' Jake added. 'Look at me. I never thought I'd get married, yet here I am.'

She smiled. 'You're just the same. The only difference is now you've got two women to keep you in check.'

'Mel said she's going to need all the advice you can give her.'

'Mel doesn't need advice. She took the measure of you the first day you met.'

'I still need you and Sam.'

'You can't get rid of us just by getting married.'

'As long as we're clear.' He squeezed her shoulder. 'So, are you going to be all right?'

Jenny's lips twisted. 'That depends on how long Matt stays in town.'

'How long is he staying?'

'He hasn't said.' She bit her lip. 'I want him to leave.'

'He did that once already,' Jake reminded her gently.

'I've got a good job, good friends,' Jenny said desperately, 'and the best little boy anyone could want.'

'Not so little anymore and not so easy.'

'I don't need Matt's help.' She swallowed hard. 'He didn't trust me, Jake.'

'He was young back then.'

'I was young too.' She stared into her friend's eyes. 'He can't waltz back here now and expect to be a father.' Or make love to her again, however good that might feel. She touched her tongue to her lips, could almost imagine the imprint of Matt's mouth.

'Things change,' Jake said again.

'People don't.'

'You used to think he was perfect.'

'Matt's not perfect.' Although he had perfect eyes, perfect lips, and a perfect body. She had thought his heart was perfect, too. 'I'm not giving him the chance to hurt my son.'

'Are you talking about me?'

Jenny swirled around, and found Matt behind her.

Jake landed a kiss on Jenny's cheek. 'I've got to go.'

'Don't go,' Jenny begged.

'Mel needs me to cut the cake.'

'You've already done that.'

'Take off her garter, then, or help her throw the bouquet.' He gave Jenny a swift hug. 'Think about what I said.' Then he clapped Matt across his back and slipped away in the direction of his bride.

Jenny watched him go, felt her lifeline disappear.

A drum roll sounded. Jenny gazed dazedly to where Jake joined Melissa. Her friend was married now, was about to depart on his honeymoon. She could no longer depend on his support.

The drum rolled again. Mel turned so she stood with her back to the crowd, and her arm arced up and over her head. From her hand an object flew straight toward Jenny.

Without thinking, Jenny lifted her hand, tried to ward off the projectile before it hit her in the face. Her fingers closed around the velvety petals of roses.

The bride's bouquet.

She had caught the bouquet.

If Matt hadn't been here, she and Jake could have laughed, could have joked about him someday introducing her to her future husband. She didn't feel like joking now. Not when Matt was by her side, the man with whom she'd once expected to walk down the aisle and proclaim everlasting love before family and friends.

Love with Matt Chambers didn't last as long as it took to grow a child in her womb.

Jenny's fingers straightened. She dropped the bouquet. Matt's hand flashed out and caught the roses before they fell.

The wedding guests cheered, and some cried out, as though she and Matt were two Christians in the Coliseum, there to entertain the Romans with their deaths. It was obvious from the cheers, that people wanted them to kiss.

Jenny glanced to her right, expecting to find Matt as reluctant as her. Instead she found him smiling his lopsided smile and in his eyes there lurked a challenge.

She squared her shoulders. Jake's guests could cheer until the rose petals died and fluttered to the floor like drops of blood, could clink spoons against tea cups until they shattered with sound, but the last thing she would ever allow again was Matt Chambers' lips on her own.

Then Matt did what he had done before, claiming her mouth with decisive action. Jenny's impulse to pull away was stifled by the heat and power of the kiss, and the remembered passion printed on her soul.

With a final cheer, the crowd shifted their attention back to Jake and Melissa, following them outside to see them off on their first married journey.

Jenny stayed where she was. Matt didn't move either, except to hold out the bouquet to her.

'I don't want it,' she said, clenching her hands to her side.

'You caught it,' he replied.

'I didn't mean to.' The time was past for her to stand next to Matt and clutch a bridal bouquet.

He laid the flowers on a nearby table. 'Then let's talk.'

Her throat turned dry.

'But not here,' Matt went on. 'Come on. I'll take you home.'

'I'm not going with you.'

'I thought the point of sending Sam away was so the grown-ups could talk.'

If they were the grown-ups, why didn't she feel measured and mature?

'Or are you afraid?'

He had accused her once before of being afraid when he first asked her out and she had said no.

She had been afraid of his eyes that saw deep into hers, afraid of the feelings coursing through her body. Afraid of how much she wanted to be with him, for he was a football star, a *catch*, while she was an inexperienced sophomore, a *nobody*.

Her mother, too, had frightened her by warning her that boys only wanted one thing. And with Matt Chambers, that's what she wanted also.

Which made him dangerous. She had to steer clear.

She had more to lose now than simple virginity.

Swiftly, she turned and raced out the door, losing herself in the crowd surrounding Jake and Mel. Then spying a cab standing at the curb, she threw herself in it and roared alone down the drive.

7

Jenny fought Sam's baseball pants into the dryer, grimacing at the grass stains still streaking the knees. No other moms of the players on Sam's team seemed to be stain-challenged the way she was. Although the other moms probably didn't allow a dirty uniform to lie under their sons' beds for six weeks.

Life was so hectic she hadn't even noticed that they hadn't turned in the uniform at the end of the season. Besides which, she hated doing laundry. But standing and feeding clothes into the machine was better than thinking of the man she had vowed to forget.

Sam had been in bed by the time she got home. She had peeked into his room and watched him breathe, had remembered the times she'd done that when he was little, when she had feared his asthma might stop his breathing, had feared she'd be unable to keep her son safe.

Where had Matt been then?

She gathered up the clean pile of Sam's clothes and marveled at how suddenly big they seemed. It didn't matter how old her son got, the struggle to keep him safe was getting harder.

Sam seemed to question everything she said, telling her on a daily basis that she was out of the loop. She wasn't even sure which loop she was out of. She just wished she could find the way back in. Matt would probably know the entrance by instinct for he had always been the epitome of cool.

Jenny pressed her lips tight and mounted the stairs to the main floor. She'd phone Vivian next and cancel dinner. She should have done it last night, but Vivian would have demanded to know why she wasn't coming, would deride her concerns about meeting with Matt. Vivian didn't know, and Jenny didn't want to tell her, that Matt was the father of her son.

Jenny climbed the next flight of stairs to the second story and laid Sam's clean clothes on his bed. She almost didn't hear the doorbell as she bent to retrieve a wet towel from his floor. She straightened. It rang again.

Jenny glanced at her watch. Eleven o'clock already. Sam shouldn't be home yet, but if he was, why was he ringing the bell to get in? He must have forgotten his key again. She hurried from his room and went down the stairs, smiling as she put her hand on the front door knob. Despite her son's desire to believe he was grown up, he still had some of his little boy ways. She loved those ways, didn't want him to lose them, didn't want either to have the bond between them break.

Which would surely happen if Matt told Sam the truth.

'Hey Sam,' she said, opening the door.

'Not Sam,' Matt replied, standing there before her on her front porch.

'Go away.' She tried to slam the door in his face.

He put out his hand and stopped her. 'We have to talk.'

'We talked enough yesterday.'

'We haven't even begun.' He looked over her shoulder. 'Where's Sam?'

'He's not here. He's at a friend's.'

'Then I'll wait.' Without asking permission, he stepped inside.

Jenny tried to block his progress, but it was like trying to block a bull charging through a chute. 'You can't wait,' she said desperately as he moved down the hall and into the living room.

He turned, didn't sit, as she assumed he would, on one of the two armchairs facing the sofa. 'We need to figure out what happened.'

'It happened so long ago it doesn't matter anymore.' It had mattered every day of her life since then, but to tell Matt that would give him power, and Matt had enough power already.

'We have a son together. It matters.'

She felt as though she was going to

be sick. 'I got pregnant,' she said. 'You weren't interested.'

'That's not true.' Matt's jaw line tightened. 'When you told me you were pregnant, I was scared. Anyone would be. But I was also thrilled. We might have been young, but I'd have given anything to have a child with you.'

'But you didn't give anything. All you did was leave.'

'I told you why. I didn't think Sam was mine.'

Any air she had left fled her lungs. 'The only man I'd ever made love to was you.'

'That's not what I heard.'

'So you said back then.' In words that were written in neon on her brain.

His eyes turned black, as though frozen into ice, the sort of ice that spins cars off the road. As she was spinning, right here, right now.

'You accused me,' she went on, vainly attempting to order her tumbling thoughts, 'of sleeping around.'

His back was ramrod straight, his legs

straight also. 'In many ways I couldn't blame you. You deserved more attention. I wasn't able to give you enough of my time.'

'I didn't want attention. All I wanted was you.'

'You had me,' he said, then glanced away, as though attempting to buy time to marshal his thoughts. Slowly, he turned back to her. 'Which is why I didn't understand how you could throw away what we had.'

'What made you think I did?'

His feet shifted then and he moved toward the fireplace. He touched a photo there. 'A bunch of things,' he finally said.

'What sort of things?'

'There was a party.' He turned and faced her. 'You know the one I'm talking about. It was after the game against Portland.'

'I hated those parties.' She had only endured them to be with him.

'You were dressed in that black skirt, the one that was short and tight across the bum, with a slit up the side to the top of your legs.'

Her lips twisted down. 'I got a friend to help me choose that skirt. I had to hide the fact from my mother that I bought it.' Who had seemed determined to ruin any social life Jenny might have by buying her sensible clothes and shoes.

'It was sexy,' Matt said, in a husky voice. 'All the guys thought so.'

'I was wearing it for you.' She had loved that skirt, had packed it in her book bag, only bringing it out once she arrived at school. She had slipped into the girls' wash room and changed her clothes when no one was around.

'I thought it was cool,' Jenny added. She hadn't wanted the other girls to see what she had to go through in order to look cool. She already knew exactly what they thought, that someone like her didn't deserve a boy like Matt.

She had been an idiot, so young, so naive.

'Every time I went to get you a

drink,' Matt went on, 'you'd be flirting with some other guy by the time I got back.'

'I didn't even know how to flirt.'

Pain surfaced in Matt's eyes. 'Then you did it by instinct.'

'I thought you wanted me to fit in,' Jenny cried. 'I didn't want you ashamed of being with me, of being the only guy there with a shy and nerdy girlfriend.'

'You weren't nerdy,' he said, 'and I liked it that you were shy.'

'You were the football star, the great hope of the whole city.'

'What has that got to do with anything?'

Her old fears flooded back, the insecurities, the uncertainty. 'You could have had your pick of anyone in the school — a cheerleader, a party girl, someone who was popular.'

'If I'd wanted one of the other girls, I would have asked her out instead of you.'

'None of those girls were like me or my friends.' They didn't know the agony of being on the outside. 'I decided if I was going to fit in, I'd better watch the other girls and do what they did.'

'I can't believe you wanted to be like *them*.'

'I didn't want you to get bored.'

His expression softened. 'I liked you just as you were. You were beautiful.'

'Not so much.'

'And funny.' He smiled as though remembering how they had laughed.

'Bumbling would be more on the mark.'

'And you were sweet.'

'I didn't want to be sweet.'

Matt shook his head. 'It was so long ago.' He turned and picked up the photo this time, not really looking at it, just turning it in his hands. 'But it wasn't just about what I saw. I was told you had slept with other people. My teammates,' he added.

'Who told you that?'

'It doesn't matter.'

'Of course it matters.' She couldn't

control the outrage in her voice, or the new pain now shafting through her. 'I never slept with anyone but you.'

His hands dropped to his sides, the photo with them. 'You kissed Todd Masterson and Randy Green.'

'They kissed me. It was just a kiss.'

'Randy said you slept with them both the weekend I was away checking out Florida State. I asked Todd about it, too, and he didn't deny it.'

'Those boys never denied a potential conquest in their lives. Did you ever think they might have been jealous?'

He frowned. 'Of what?'

'Of you, of course. You'd just won your scholarship. Your future was bright.'

Matt looked stunned, as though suddenly he, also, found the past too present. He swept his hair back from his forehead. 'It could have happened like that. But then why would Coach Ramsey say it was true?'

'Did he say that? How would he know?' It was too late for despair, but pain filled her gut.

'Coach knew everything.'

'He didn't know this.' She glanced at her hands and saw her fingers were clenched, saw her skin turning white around the edges. 'Coach lied to you, Matt.'

'Ramsey wouldn't lie.'

'Ask him,' she said, lifting her chin.

'I will.' He drew in a giant breath. 'But you did lie. You know you did.'

She hadn't considered it a lie at the time, but had regretted it ever since.

'You told me Phil wasn't your boyfriend.'

'We'd only been out a couple of times. Phil was the son of my mother's best friend.' He'd been nice-looking and well-mannered, but with little sex appeal. 'My mother made me go out with him.'

'So why didn't you say that when I asked?'

Jenny caught her breath, didn't want to look pathetic. 'I was afraid,' she finally said. 'I thought that if you knew I was dating someone else, you wouldn't ask me out.' Her face felt tight as though she wore a mask. 'I wanted you to like me.'

'I did like you.'

'Not enough to stick with me,' she said softly. 'Not enough to trust me.'

His expression hardened. 'I'd learned not to trust. My father — '

'What?'

'He lied, too. His whole life was a lie.'

She wanted to touch him, to erase the hurt from his eyes, but his body stiffened and the moment passed.

'It doesn't matter,' he said again. 'But why,' he demanded, 'did you get so angry when I confronted you with what I learned from Coach?'

'Do you blame me?' she asked.

'I thought you were just trying to cover the truth. I still wanted you, needed you, but you wouldn't explain anything.'

'I was too angry.' It made her angry even now, remembering that moment.

'I walked around for ages, couldn't

imagine a life without you. I decided that Coach must have got it wrong.' Matt turned back to the fireplace, and this time stared at the red dahlias she had placed in a vase in front of the cold grate, a splash of winter color on a late summer's day. 'So I came back to have it out with you.' He turned, his eyes narrowing. 'That's when I saw you with Phil. You were in his arms.'

'He was comforting me.' Jenny fought back the tears. 'He knew I was upset.'

'He was kissing your hair, acting like a lover.'

She gulped in some air. 'He was not my lover.'

'Then why did he tell me that he was?' Matt slowly placed the photo in his hand back on to the mantel.

It was a photo of her and Phil taken at their wedding. In it, Jenny was looking off into the distance, but Phil was staring straight at her.

All Jenny's strength deserted her body. She moved to the chair next to the window, and sank down into it, grateful for its support. 'He was not my lover,' she repeated.

'You married him,' Matt went on.

'Yes, but not then,' she said, lifting her head. 'Not for ages. I was pregnant don't forget. I couldn't go marrying other men.' She put her hands on the arms of her chair and used their support to slowly stand. 'It was Phil who stood by me, wanted to marry me.' He had finally worn her down into saying yes. It had taken two years, but he had persisted, had told her he didn't need her to love him back. He had enough love for both of them, he said.

But it hadn't been enough. And despite Phil lying to Matt, he deserved better, deserved a woman who loved him as a lover, not with the less passionate love of a friend.

If she married again, it would be to get the best. For her and for Sam. For the husband she chose.

8

He had always intended to visit Coach Ramsey, but not like this, not armed with a list of whys and wherefores. The old man had never liked inquisitions, had expected his boys to simply do as they were told.

And his players were happy to do just that, for they knew Coach always worked for their benefit. He had done for them what no other coach had. He had taken their school to the State Championships and on to victory. For a no-name high school that was no mean feat.

Sure the man was hard, made them work like Trojans, but the blood, sweat and pain made them appreciate their success. If it hadn't been for Coach, he would never have got his full ride, would never have made it to play in the National Football League. Coach had set him up for life.

Which made it impossible to believe that Coach would ever have lied about Jenny.

The gym smelled the same, still musty with old sweat, but when Matt knocked and stepped into Coach's office, he couldn't believe how old Coach looked. Much smaller than the imposing figure he remembered, or maybe it was just that he himself had grown up.

'Hey, Coach,' Matt said.

The old man opposite lifted a head of cropped white hair. 'Matt Chambers!' he exclaimed, and rose stiffly to his feet. He reached for Matt's hand and gripped it hard. 'Good to see you. I knew you'd be in town for Jake's wedding. Wondered how long it would take you to come see me.'

'I had a few things to take care of first.'

'How's the leg?' Coach asked, peering over his glasses down Matt's length.

'It's fine,' Matt answered. 'Healing nicely.'

Coach's eyes lit up. 'Will you get back to playing?'

'Nope, that's over.'

'Hm,' Coach grunted. 'So what are you going to do? I heard both the Dolphins and the Seahawks want you on their coaching staff.'

'News travels fast.'

'Either team would be great. But what's this rumor I hear about you working with kids? That's a job for old-timers like me.'

'I like kids,' Matt said. 'I'm thinking of working with some inner-city boys mostly.'

'Any prospects amongst them?'

'I'm not looking for prospects.'

'Don't bullshit me, boy. Coaches always look for players.'

'Maybe,' Matt said, 'but I'm more concerned that these boys get through childhood alive.'

'I heard you started up some sort of foundation for football scholarships.'

'That's right. It's for players with good academics and no money. They

114

don't have to be stars. They just have to really want to go to college.'

'You were a star.'

Matt smiled. 'That's not what you told me when I was in high school.'

'Didn't want to swell your head,' Coach said gruffly. 'I wanted you to work.'

'I worked all right. There was hardly time for anything else.'

'That's right, that's right.' Coach nodded his head. 'That's what I keep telling my boys. Forget about the girls and goofing off. You've got to work if you're going to make it.' He slapped Matt on his back. 'Like you did, boy!'

'I had a girlfriend.' Matt watched Coach closely.

'So you did. A pretty little tart.'

Matt stiffened. 'Not a tart.'

'No? Didn't she get pregnant?'

'It takes two to get pregnant.'

Coach turned and moved back behind his desk. 'You were best off without her. Girls are a dime a dozen. You must have discovered that by now.'

'Jenny was one in a million. That's what I discovered.'

Coach lowered himself heavily into his chair.

'I came to you,' Matt went on, 'when Jenny told me she was pregnant.'

'Smartest move you ever made.'

Matt couldn't bring himself to sit in the chair opposite. 'You said the baby wasn't mine.'

'Could've been anyone's.'

'You said you knew Jenny had been sleeping around.'

Coach looked at him hard. 'Someone had to say it.' His blue eyes had faded, but the steel they'd once had still shone through. 'What does it matter?'

'It matters to me.' Matt took a step closer. 'I'm asking why you said it.'

'Someone had to get you out of that mess. That girl and her baby were about to drag you down.'

'It was my baby, too.'

'We couldn't let it be yours.'

It suddenly seemed to Matt that his breathing had stopped, that he'd been

116

running stairs and was now out of air. 'What do you mean we couldn't let it be mine?'

'You had just got your scholarship.' Coach smiled at him proudly. 'You were the first one in our school to ever get a full ride. The first student of mine!'

The pain in Matt's lungs extended to his chest. 'So you decided to lie.'

'I had to,' he said. 'You were sweet on that blonde girlie. No telling what you'd do if you thought her baby was yours.'

'I'd have taken care of her.' And he would have taken care of his baby. In a way his father had never done for him. Matt swallowed past the lump in his throat. 'I came to you because I trusted you to help figure out some way of handling the situation.'

'And that's what I did. You could never have gone to Florida with a wife and baby in tow.'

'Then I wouldn't have gone.'

'Exactly. Now you're getting it. I couldn't let such a thing happen.'

Coach leaned forward, his gaze pinning Matt's. 'We were all counting on you, boy. To get a scholarship player coming out of Kent High meant money in our school's sports coffers for years to come.'

'You told me lies for the benefit of a high school sports program?'

'Hell no, boy. It was for you. And for your family. You would never have got to university otherwise.'

'I would have worked, would have saved my tuition. I would have got there somehow.'

'And what about football? I couldn't just let you throw away your future. What the hell kind of a coach would I have been then?'

Matt worked hard to control the urge to throttle the old man. 'That wasn't your decision. My son's twelve now, Coach. Twelve! I've missed twelve years.'

'Count yourself lucky you missed that baby stage. Bloody hard work. What about the kid now? Does he play ball like you? What high school does he plan to attend?'

Wavy lines had formed in front of Matt's eyes and it felt as though his head was about to explode. He had missed it all right, every precious moment of Sam's childhood. And that was due in part to the man standing before him.

And to himself, for being stupid, for not seeing what he should have seen — that the Coach he had trusted had lied to him big time. The guys had, too, while Jenny was the only one telling the truth.

It wasn't just to Sam that he needed to make amends.

★   ★   ★

'You're back,' Jenny said when she opened the door, her expression exhibiting her dismay. 'I thought we said all we needed to say this morning.'

'We've only just begun. Can I come in?'

She didn't say he could, simply stood there uncertainly, as though he were a ghost back to haunt her.

Matt's gut twisted. Jenny had every right to hate him for what he had done. It had all been such a mess back then. He gritted his jaw. 'I'm sorry,' he said.

'Sorry doesn't help.'

'What will?'

'Nothing. Just go away.'

'I'm not going anywhere. I have to see Sam.'

'Why?' she asked.

'I need to tell him I'm his father.'

'No!' Her face turned pale.

'We can't keep it a secret.'

'Even if it hurts your son?'

Matt's heart leaped as the words *your son* escaped her lips. 'Sam deserves the truth,' he said firmly.

Jenny turned away. 'He doesn't even know you.'

He touched her shoulder and pulled her around to face him. 'We'll get to know each other.'

'Before you tell him?'

Matt gazed hard into Jenny's eyes. 'If that's the way you want it.'

'How long do you think getting to know him will take?'

'I don't know. A day or two?' He had already felt a connection between them.

Jenny looked pityingly at him. 'I've known Sam since the day he was born and he's still a mystery to me. Kids his age are from another planet.'

'Then it might take longer. But I do have experience with boys, you know.' Excitement shafted through him. Now he'd be doing things with his own son. 'You have to trust me, Jenny.'

'Exactly,' she said, placing her hands on her hips and looking as though that would never happen.

'He needs to know,' Matt insisted. 'We'll tell him tomorrow.'

'And if I don't want to?'

'I'll do it myself.'

'Then I won't let you see him.'

'He'll be at Vivian's tonight.'

'Sam and I won't go.'

From behind Jenny came the sound of footsteps pounding up the back stairs. Her blue eyes widened. 'Promise me,' she begged, 'that you won't just tell him. Promise you'll let me decide when and if the moment's right.'

Then a door slammed and Sam erupted into the hall behind Jenny.

'I'm home, Mom,' he hollered, kicking off his shoes.

Matt met Jenny's gaze and saw the worry there, the desperation.

She turned towards her son. 'Hi, honey, I'm glad you're home.'

Sam stared past his mother and his eyes lit up.

'Hey, sport,' Matt said, then gave himself a mental kick. Nobody used the word *sport* anymore. No one had used it even in his day, unless that person was over a hundred.

'You remember Mr. Chambers don't you, Sam?'

'Of course I remember him, and his name is Matt.'

'That's right,' Matt said, smiling.

Which caused Jenny's frown to deepen.

He didn't like to see her frown and know he had caused it, especially when his presence used to give her joy. Her joy had made him happy. He missed that feeling, hadn't realized how much.

'What's up?' Sam asked.

'I thought you and your mom might like a ride over to Vivian and John's.'

'Cool,' Sam said.

'No, thank you,' Jenny cried.

'In my '53 Chieftain,' Matt added, with another smile.

'Wow!' Sam raced past him and stepped out onto the front porch. He peered down the street. 'Wow!' he said again. 'An antique car! How come you parked so far away?'

'Your driveway was blocked.'

'That's Mr. Hanson's RV,' Sam explained. 'He's away right now so he left it with us. Figured kids might mess with it if they knew he wasn't home.'

'It was nice of you to let him keep it here.'

'Mr. Hanson's a good guy.'

'We don't need a ride,' Jenny said.

Matt turned to face her.

'Sam and I aren't able to stay for long. There's no reason for you to cut your visit short.'

'Aw, mom,' Sam said. 'I want to go with Matt.'

'If you come with me,' Matt said to Jenny, 'we could go for coffee afterwards.'

'All of us?' Sam asked.

'Not this time, pal. Your mom and I have a lot of catching up to do.'

'You're going out?' Sam asked, his eyes incredulous. 'On a date?'

'No,' Jenny denied.

'Yes,' Matt replied.

Sam wrinkled his nose. 'My mom doesn't date.'

'Never?' Matt asked.

'Never,' the boy assured him. 'She's old,' he added.

'I am not old,' Jenny protested.

'She is,' Sam insisted.

Matt chuckled. 'Then I guess that

makes me over the hill.'

'Nope, you still play sports. And you're a guy.' Sam grinned at his mother. 'Guys don't get old as quickly as girls.'

'Right,' Jenny said, 'that's enough.' She pointed to Sam. 'Get your Science Fair project together and let's get going if we're going to go.'

'With Matt, right?'

'I guess so,' Jenny said, 'but we're not staying long. And I'm not going for coffee after.'

'Old people don't stay up later than nine o'clock,' Sam taunted as he turned and raced to get his stuff.

'Stop laughing,' Jenny ordered.

'Hard not to,' Matt said.

She waited until Sam had disappeared up the stairs. 'What were you thinking?' she demanded, 'telling Sam we have a date?'

'I had to tell him something. You didn't want me to tell him that he's my son.'

'You could have said something else.'

She frowned. 'Anything else.'

'Why are you so uncomfortable? Was Sam right? Do you never date?'

'I wouldn't say never.'

'A woman like you should be surrounded by men.' She looked so damned good to him, all soft curves and even softer skin.

'I haven't had time for men,' Jenny said firmly. 'Bringing up a child is a full time job.'

'I'm here to help.' He took a step closer, could smell her perfume, and under the perfume, the sweet scent of her skin.

She took a step back.

'Trust me,' he said again.

* * *

Trust was not something she'd ever done lightly, and was especially not something she intended to do with Matt, in spite of the way he'd charmed everyone at dinner.

She wished she could attribute her

son being impressed to the passion Sam felt for all things wheeled, but the reality was Matt held everyone's attention with the stories he told of his football career.

He'd even made her forget for the course of a meal that he'd done her so wrong it could never be fixed.

She peeked through the door into the kitchen and saw Matt with his hands in the washing-up water, talking to John as though they were best friends.

'Why don't you just go in there and grab him?' Vivian suggested from her chair next to their record player.

'Grab him?' Jenny said.

'Put your hands on his chest, run your fingers through his hair, take him by the hand and run off into the night.' Vivian grinned at Jenny and blew her a kiss. 'Admit it, girlfriend. You like the guy!' She picked up a record and peered at the label. 'And I intend to take all of the credit. Without me you two wouldn't have had a chance to talk, let alone do other things.'

'We've done other things,' Jenny muttered under her breath, and although she liked to think Sam had turned out well, single parenthood was not an experiment she wished to repeat.

'What's that?' Vivian asked, taking another record from the shelf.

'I said matchmaking's not your thing.'

'You couldn't have spent the evening with a more perfect man! Not only is he cute, he's rich to boot.'

'How do you know that?'

'He's one of the best professional quarterbacks in the country.'

'He's injured now. He's not going back.'

'He's done a ton of endorsements, he'll be coaching a pro team, probably owning a piece of one, he has a house in Florida, an apartment in Manhattan, he drives a vintage car, and he's staying at the best hotel in Seattle.'

Jenny laughed. 'Where did you get all that information?'

'The internet, of course.' Vivian

placed the record she had chosen in the player. 'And what the internet didn't say simply required a few choice questions of the man himself.'

'Why didn't I hear you asking all those questions?'

'I asked them when Matt came with me to the basement to choose the wine for dinner. Another thing he's good at,' Vivian added triumphantly.

Jenny smiled. 'You've only got two kinds of wine, my friend — red and white — and of such dubious vintage you've taken the labels off.'

'We didn't take them off,' Vivian said ruefully. 'That happened last winter when the water heater burst. I told John to move the cases away from the heater, but would he listen? Besides,' her friend went on, 'Matt bought a couple of very expensive wines. I recognized their names from when I used to work at the ad agency.'

'You're not sorry you quit?' Jenny asked, needing to talk about something other than Matt Chambers.

Vivian sighed. 'Not really. Not usually. Not when it's the weekend and I know I wouldn't normally be going to work that day.'

'I really don't understand why you quit work just to get pregnant.'

'It was John's idea. He's very old-fashioned for a modern guy. He doesn't want me to keep working once we produce his son and heir, and he reckons if I get used to being a lady of leisure, I'll never want to go back.'

'Is he right?' Jenny asked. She envied Vivian. Spending time with a baby was an unequaled joy. She wished she'd had more time to spend with Sam.

Vivian grinned. 'I told him he'd better get a second job then, because the lap of luxury doesn't come cheap. All this laying around makes me realize what's important. Money,' she said, poking her finger into Jenny's chest, 'and, even better, a cute guy with money.'

'You know you don't mean that!'

'Don't mean what?'

130

Jenny turned her head at the sound of Matt's voice. He and John had finished the dishes and were moving into the living room. Heat hit Jenny's cheeks. How long had Matt been there? Had he heard their conversation? 'Where's Sam?' she asked, ignoring Matt's question.

'Gluing odd shaped bits on to his science project,' Matt replied.

'Is he at that stage already? Does he need any help?'

'He says he wants to do it on his own.'

'I thought you were going to help him?'

'I gave him some pointers.' Matt flopped down onto the sofa beside her. 'Helping doesn't mean doing the project for him.'

'When I help it does,' Jenny admitted.

'Matt obviously has the magic touch with children.' Vivian cast an I-told-you-so glance at Jenny.

'The perfect man,' Jenny murmured.

131

'Did you just call me perfect?' Matt asked, with a grin.

Jenny shook her head. 'You're far from perfect.'

'So,' Vivian said suddenly, turning back to Matt. 'Do you want kids some day?'

Jenny's pulse began thudding against her temple.

'Don't toy with the man!' John said, frowning at his wife. 'Why not just come right out and ask him what his intentions are towards Jenny?'

Jenny groaned. 'This is why I never bring anyone to your house. This is why I don't even mention if I go out on a date.'

'I thought you didn't date?' Matt said with a straight face.

'Not anymore if this is what it's like.'

Matt laughed out loud, his baritone resonating off the high ceilings. Then he turned to Jenny and his laughter died. 'Yes,' he said, staring into her eyes. 'I would like to have children.'

Jenny's heart slammed to a stop.

When Matt said he wanted children, what did he mean? Did he intend to seek custody of her son?

No court in the land would countenance such a thing.

Unless the courts were swayed by money and power.

Of which she had little, while he had a lot.

Jenny rose to her feet, suddenly feeling faint. 'It's time Sam and I went home.'

'We haven't had dessert yet,' Vivian protested.

'I don't need dessert, and Sam has school in the morning.' Jenny sucked in a breath, prayed her friend would understand.

John looked at his watch. 'It's only seven thirty.' He glanced at Jenny, then at Matt. 'Why don't you two go out on this date Sam mentioned, and we'll get the boy home.'

Jenny shook her head.

'At least let Sam finish gluing his project,' Vivian insisted. 'If it's moved before the glue dries, it'll all fall to pieces.'

Jenny's heart sank. There was truth in what Vivian said.

'We can go if you're ready, Jenny,' Matt offered.

He looked as innocent as a babe, yet all the while he was probably composing the speech he'd make in court to convince the authorities to give him her son.

'I'll help Sam gather up his stuff.' Matt stood and smiled his thanks to Vivian and John. 'I don't have room for dessert anyway. I was hoping no one would notice, but I ate two helpings of roast beef.'

Jenny's head began to throb. What was Matt doing? He had said that he wanted to get her alone to talk, and now here he was including Sam.

'I've changed my mind.' She turned to John and Vivian. 'If you're sure you don't mind taking Sam home after he glues his project, I will go out and have coffee with Matt. You don't need to stay with Sam until I get home, Vivian. I won't be late.'

Vivian stood and hugged her, then whispered in her ear as she walked Jenny to the door. 'Hang on to this one, girlfriend. The man is a keeper.'

Hanging on hadn't helped thirteen years before. Hanging on was not what she intended to do now.

9

Nor was getting answers she thought she wanted to questions that had been gnawing since she met Matt again. Perhaps it was best just to keep things simple.

Jenny glanced at Matt and felt a stab of worry. She knew from the past that when his brows met, his mind was working overtime and his thoughts were dark.

In high school those thoughts usually revolved around football and which sequence of plays would win the league final. She knew that sports weren't on his mind now.

It was raining again, the perfect sort of night to enjoy the coffee bar near her house. Plush chairs, warm wood tables, low lamps set around — a home away from home was what the Coffee Café was — a place where friends met and laughed over their day.

Only she and Matt weren't laughing, not like they used to, when anything and everything struck them as funny. Jenny took off her coat and hung it over the back of her chair.

Matt ceased his perusal of the coffee bar's menu and his brow smoothed. 'I haven't had good coffee since I left Seattle.'

'Try the mocha latte,' Jenny suggested. 'I think I've become addicted.'

'Your coffee used to be good.'

'I never made you coffee.'

'I remember you inviting me over for some once.'

Heat flooded Jenny's face as she remembered that day. They had ended up in her bedroom while her parents were out, kissing each other with teenage hunger.

If they made love now, it would be different . . . more passionate, more mature, than it had been before. But making love to Matt was now out of the picture, for they were no longer

137

teenagers in love. They had hurt each other, had caused each other pain.

'What would *you* like?' Matt asked suddenly.

'Some answers,' she replied.

'A mocha latte?' he said.

'Not those kind of answers.'

His eyebrows lifting, he called to the youth behind the counter and placed their order.

'How long are you staying?' she demanded, when their drinks were set down steaming in front of them.

'However long it takes.' He leaned back in his chair, assured and relaxed, as though she was his girl and they were truly on a date.

'To do what?' she asked, her mouth turning dry.

'To get to know my son.'

'He likes baseball, not football, likes to read, but not listen, and he doesn't need a father in his life.'

'Every boy needs a father.'

'Then you should have been there from the day he was born.'

'I'm here now,' he said quietly, a flicker of something passing over his face.

Vulnerability? Regret? Jenny couldn't tell. It came and went with a speed that caught her breath.

'I made a mistake,' Matt went on. 'I listened to Coach. I trusted my eyes. Should have listened to my heart and what it said.'

'What do you mean?' Jenny leaned towards him across the table, tried to read his eyes in the subdued light of the coffee bar.

'I never forgot you, even after I believed you had betrayed me.'

She, too, had tried to drive Matt from her heart, but now he was back, she knew she hadn't succeeded.

'But there's no point,' he went on, 'in rehashing all that. We're here to talk about how we can go forward.'

Jenny's heart clenched. Here's where he would tell her just what he intended. Here's where her life as she knew it would be over.

'I've missed thirteen years,' he went on in a low voice. 'All the birthdays, first steps, first words, everything. I can't miss any more.'

If she had missed those years, she'd feel the same way. Sympathy sprung in her breast and she swallowed hard. 'So what are you proposing?'

'That you and I work something out. That we set up times for me to see Sam.'

If she was Matt, she would never rest until she got access. But what if she was right and he wanted something more? What if he wanted to take her son from her?

'I want to see him, Jenny,' he insisted. 'It's only right.'

Jenny shut her eyes and wished she could will herself back to her own home, with all her own safe, familiar things around her.

'Well?' Matt said.

Jenny opened her eyes and faced him head on. 'I'll agree to you seeing him, but not alone.'

'What are you afraid of?'

That Sam would love Matt just as she had once done.

Matt frowned. 'I'm not going to try and steal him.'

It seemed ridiculous when put like that, but when she'd seen Matt at Jake's wedding, so tall and so strong, so power-filled, she had been afraid of what he might do. If he didn't physically carry away her son, he had seemed entirely capable of emotionally capturing him.

Especially when the minute Sam met him, her son's eyes had filled with hero-worship. If Matt offered Sam the world as he once did her, how could Sam say no?

'Sam's at a vulnerable age right now,' she replied.

'I understand that. I'll go softly . . . softly.'

'I don't think you know what softly, softly means.'

'What can go wrong? Until you feel more comfortable, you'll be there all the time. We'll pretend to be dating. Sam won't know I'm there for him.'

She caught her breath.

He reached for her hand. 'Which means we have to be nice to each other.'

Jenny snatched her hand away. 'We're not actually dating, and what do you mean by *nice*?'

He smiled into her eyes. 'This feels like a date, and by nice I mean we're not allowed to fight. We can talk, laugh . . . we can have a good time.' He lifted his hand airily. 'Do what dating couples do.'

Jenny grimaced. 'I think I've forgotten.'

'Take my hand,' Matt instructed.

Reluctantly, she did.

The minute he touched her fingers, he knew that he had made a mistake. The purpose of the exercise was to get to know his son, not physically connect with the woman he'd once loved.

Perhaps it was the wine he'd drunk earlier at John and Vivian's or maybe it

142

was the ambiance of the cozy cafe they were in, but touching Jenny's hand felt good.

If he felt like this at a mere touch, how in the hell was he ever going to kiss her? And he had to kiss her. That was what dating couples did.

He squeezed her hand.

She pulled away.

'Relax,' he said. 'We're not doing anything wrong.'

'You're touching me.'

'Yes.'

'We're in the middle of a café.'

'Would you prefer we go out to the car?'

The shock in her eyes hit him, made him realize what he had just said. The first time they'd made love they had been in the Chieftain.

'Don't worry,' he went on hastily. 'I'm not suggesting anything drastic. We're not exactly on the same wavelength as those two.' He gestured toward a young couple on a neighboring love seat, who were ignoring their drinks in favor of exploring each other's mouths.

Jenny glanced at them also then just as swiftly averted her gaze. 'I wonder what that girl's mother would say if she saw her.'

'Exactly the question I asked myself when I was their age.'

Jenny chuckled.

'It's good to hear you laugh.' Matt gestured again to the teenaged pair. 'That's what we're going to have to do.'

'Laughing's one thing,' Jenny said, 'but I have no intention of kissing you.'

'How else are we going to be convincing as a dating couple?'

'The only person we have to convince is Sam, and I'm not kissing you in front of him.'

'Other couples would.'

'I don't care. Sam has never seen me kissing a man.'

'Surely he saw you and your husband kiss?' Matt took a sip of coffee and tried to seem nonchalant but really he was watching her closely.

'That's different and you know it. Besides, Sam wouldn't remember. He was only four when Phil died.'

'What about Jake and John?'

'They're friends. When I kiss them, I don't kiss them like that.'

'Like what?' he teased. 'Could be you've forgotten how to kiss.'

She flushed a deep pink.

Kissing Jenny would be a pleasure. Stopping would be the problem. It had certainly been a problem when they were younger.

'Knowing how to kiss is like riding a bike,' Jenny said briskly.

'A little easier on the butt.'

She chuckled again.

'How about we practice?' he suggested.

'We don't need practice.'

He stared down at their now separated hands. 'We can at least hold hands.'

'Holding hands is over-rated.'

Not when it was Jenny's hand he was holding. The pleasure of her touch would stay in his mind for hours. But before he could reach for her, she reached for him, and slowly, with great show, placed her hand in his.

He closed his fingers around hers. 'Practice is good.'

'Maybe,' she replied.

'Although you've got to loosen up.' He scrutinized her face. 'You seem a little tense.'

'I am tense.'

'Roll your shoulders,' he suggested. 'That'll relax your muscles.'

'It's hard to roll my shoulders with my arms stretched out like this.'

'Then come over and sit by me.' He pulled her drink to his side of the table.

'You're in a chair,' she said scathingly. 'Where exactly do you expect me to sit?'

'There's room on my lap.'

'I'm not sitting on your lap.'

'I dare you,' he replied.

'People our age don't sit on one another's laps.'

'I'm only thirty. How old are you?'

He knew to the day how old Jenny was. In school she had been two years behind him, and her seventeenth birthday had come shortly after they met.

He'd taken her to the beach and had sat next to her on a log, had presented her with a cupcake as they watched the waves roll in. He'd brought a bottle of something alcoholic, but neither had drunk more than a sip. They had gotten high on each other's company and the romance of being together in the mist of the Pacific.

His friends had teased him later about the new girl in his life, a girl no one else had noticed, but by then they were taking note. She'd been more than just pretty. She'd been sweet with it too. Her face had lit up when he entered the room.

'We're in a dark corner,' he encouraged her now. 'No one will see. I dare you,' he said again.

'I don't take dares.'

But a battle seemed to be waging

inside her head, for he could see the indecision in her eyes. Then suddenly she stood and came towards him, her perfume bringing with it the scent of the sea.

'More coffee?' she asked, just when he thought she would drop onto his lap.

'No,' he replied, taking hold of her arm.

Her nearness was heady, almost overwhelming. He tried to think of football to clear his head, but no flying pig skin or three hundred pound linebacker had anything in common with the sexy lady before him.

He rose and wrapped his arm around her shoulder. 'Ready?' he asked.

'No.'

'One, two, three, go.'

She ducked away as he leaned to kiss her, but he caught a whiff of chocolate from her drink.

'Sweet,' he said, half shutting his eyes, so didn't see her lips meet his until they were there.

'Not bad,' she said, smiling, when she

came up for air.

'You were right,' he said. 'You still remember how to kiss.' He could kick himself to hell and back. If he had trusted her before, they wouldn't be going through this charade. They'd still be together, making love all the time. And sharing Sam, the boy they had created.

'So we don't need more practice,' she whispered in his ear.

'You can never have too much practice.'

She ducked away when he tried to pull her into his arms, and glanced towards the clerk at the till. 'They'll kick us out if we start acting like teenagers.'

'If they do, they'll have no customers left.'

Her eyes widened and her gaze flew to the clock ticking away the minutes above the cappuccino machine. 'You're right. It's already ten o'clock. I've got to get home.'

'Just a few more minutes. There's

149

more to dating than kissing. We have to be comfortable when we're together. We have to act as though we like one other.'

'I always liked you,' she said softly.

'I liked you too.' More than liked. Loved. Which was why it had hurt when he had seen her with Phil.

She suddenly rose and swept up her coat from the back of her chair. 'It's time to go,' she said briskly. 'Better yet, you stay here. I'll walk home.'

'You can't walk alone.'

'What do you think I do when you're not around? My house is only two blocks away.'

He glanced through the window of the café. 'It's dark. It's not safe.'

'This is not Miami. Nothing's going to happen.'

'Then I'll walk too.' Matt grabbed his jacket and jammed his arms into it.

'What about your leg?' She looked dubiously down at his knee.

'I can still outrun you.'

Her eyebrows lifted. 'What about the Chieftain?'

'I'll walk back and get it.'

'That's crazy.'

'Maybe.' With a single smooth gesture, he drew his finger along her cheek. 'But I seem to be dating a crazy person.'

The touch felt so good she didn't want him to stop, didn't want the date to ever end. But she had to go home, had to see her son, had to get away from this man and his magic. She twisted away. 'Do what you want.'

The minute they left the Coffee Café, however, Jenny was glad Matt was with her. She loved her neighborhood, especially loved her neighbors, felt connected to the people and the place. But she didn't often go walking after dark, hadn't expected it to be quite this black.

The moon was no longer growing into fullness, was now just a sliver, not a light-filled orb. And a sliver didn't spill enough light on earth to light her path safely down the edge of the road.

There were few street lamps in this

section of town. Mr. Silverman's house was the only house that had them. He had put them in himself: four old-fashioned lamp posts lining the edge of his lawn next to the sidewalk. The lamps' round bulbs shed a welcome glow, thrusting away the shadows of the trees.

'Nice,' Matt said, gesturing toward the first lamp as they walked beneath it.

'Mr. Silverman got the posts at an auction,' Jenny explained. 'He ground off the rust and repainted them. Sam helped.'

'Sam?'

'Yes.' She glanced towards Matt. 'Sam likes working with his hands, and he likes Mr. Silverman. They poured through catalogues and brochures for ages to find the right bulbs.' Jenny smiled. Sam had seemed so grown-up then.

Matt smiled, too, but he was smiling at her.

Jenny's breath snagged, and her chest grew tight. If he kissed her again, she

152

wouldn't want to resist. His lips neared hers. She tilted up her head.

His lips were warm, hard and soft at the same time. And she could taste the coffee he'd just been drinking. His mouth roved hers, seemed to taste her also.

Her skin grew warm and, along her temple, her pulse was beating out of control. She was on her own street, in the safety of her own neighborhood, but the feelings she was experiencing were nothing short of dangerous.

Matt had hurt her once, had thrown her love in her face. But they'd both been young, both had made mistakes. Perhaps she should simply give in to the moment, live in the present instead of the past.

Then something zinged past her ear, and over her head the light bulb shattered. Glass skittered across the sidewalk. Jenny pulled away, and gazed around in stunned disbelief.

Matt pulled her back close, used his body as a shield, locking her in the safety of his embrace.

'What happened?' she cried, comforted by the steady beat of his heart. Then she heard the clatter of running feet and she twisted her head, struggling to see what had made the sound.

'Stay still,' Matt ordered, but he too looked to the other side of the street. With a frown, he said, 'Those are kids throwing stones.'

'At us?'

'It appears so.'

Jenny pulled free and peered into the darkness. 'There are four of them,' she counted, the boys' silhouettes disappearing swiftly into the shadows.

Then her heart skipped. One of the boys, the smallest of the lot, ran with a familiar up and down motion. At the corner he turned and glanced back in their direction, the light of the last lamp revealing his face.

'Sam,' Jenny breathed, her stomach heaving. She swallowed hard to fight back a rush of nausea.

'What about Sam?' Matt demanded.

She stared at him mutely, not wanting to say.

Matt searched her eyes, his own eyes darkening. 'Sam's with those boys?'

'I don't see how — ' Her brain filled with confusion, and then as though her muscles had broken free of control, she began to run in the direction the boys had gone.

It felt as though she'd already run a mile, and her head was pounding in rhythm with her heart. She couldn't believe, didn't want to *know*, that her son was with the boys vandalizing Mr. Silverman's property.

Sam couldn't, wouldn't do anything like that.

But if he hadn't done it, why was he with them?

Why couldn't she make her feet go faster? Footsteps sounded on the sidewalk behind, and Matt's hand shot out, pulling her to a halt.

'Stop,' he ordered.

'Let me go,' she answered raggedly.

'If Sam's with those boys, you don't

want to talk to him now. You'll want to do that when he's not with his friends.'

'Those boys aren't his friends.'

'Then why is he with them?'

'I . . . I don't know.' She tried to free herself. 'He should be at home. And if I wasn't out on this so-called date with a stranger, he wouldn't be running around the streets with hooligans.'

'You and I aren't strangers,' Matt contradicted her fiercely. 'We once knew each other better than anyone else.'

'It's your fault this is happening,' she said, just as fiercely.

He pressed his lips tight, seemed to be working hard to hold his anger back. 'What do you want to do?' he finally asked.

'Go home and find out what's going on.'

Matt shook his head. 'You've got to think this through. You can't just charge in hurling accusations.'

'I wasn't going to do that!' But she knew that she might have. She wanted to scream and hold Sam at the same time, wanted to turn back the clock to when he was a baby, to when she knew exactly where he was at all times.

She wanted to impress on her errant son that he couldn't roam the streets causing trouble and destruction.

For if he did that, what else would he do?

The mere contemplation of such a question turned Jenny's skin clammy. She took a deep breath, tried to ensure a steady voice. 'What do you suggest?'

'I'll go with you to your house. We'll confront Sam together.'

'What do you mean *confront*?'

'We'll ask him what he's been doing.'

Jenny blew out the air collecting in her lungs. A part of her wished Sam didn't know she had seen him. She didn't want a confrontation. Confrontation wasn't good. Not when Sam's asthma could attack at any time.

It hadn't for ages, but that could change in an instant. Sam reacted badly to stress. He could lose his breath and have to fight to get it back. When she spoke to him about what he had done, she'd have to do it in a calm and quiet manner.

'I'll talk to Sam alone,' she finally said. 'I'll ask him the questions.'

Matt's eyes locked with hers. 'Do you know those other boys?'

'Yes.' She ran her tongue over her lips, tried to create some moisture there. 'I've known two of them since they were toddlers. But they're older than Sam.'

'Did you know he was hanging about with them?'

'No,' she said, 'but I saw them the other night when I was driving home from work.'

His eyebrows lifted. 'Was Sam with them then?'

'No.'

'What were they doing?'

'Nothing much. Hanging around.' She couldn't seem to stop shaking. 'That's what boys do.'

'Does Sam do that?'

'I don't think so,' she said uncertainly. At least, she hadn't thought so. Not her son. Not her baby. But maybe Sam was right. Maybe she didn't have a clue.

'You're worried,' Matt said, his eyes also holding tension.

She'd been worried for weeks.

'Talk to me,' he demanded.

She had longed to talk to someone about her fears, either Jake or Vivian or even her parents. But she'd been afraid. If she spoke her fears would no longer be intangible and indistinct. If she spoke they might become all too real. They were real now.

'Sam's changed,' she said.

'It's called puberty,' Matt replied.

She shook her head. 'Not that kind of change. Sam doesn't seem to want to talk anymore. Or give me a hug. Or tell me things.'

Matt's expression softened. 'Boys don't when they get older. Their mother is the last person they want knowing

159

what they're thinking.'

'But he's always told me everything before. We've always been close.'

'You're still close,' Matt said reassuringly. He put his arm around her and that comforted too. 'Anyone can see that.'

Fear weighed her down. 'I've seen him a time or two, not with these boys, but with a couple of others I didn't like the look of.'

'Why? What did they look like?'

'Tough,' she answered.

'Tough?' His brows drew together.

'You know . . . tough. Big belt buckles, too-big pants, chains hanging from their pockets.'

'Have you asked Sam about his friends?'

'Not really . . . a little. I've mentioned the boys.'

He tilted his head. 'You didn't call them juvenile delinquents, I hope?'

'No.' She tried to smile, but her lips began to wobble. 'I'm not even sure they're doing anything really wrong. It's just — ' She shrugged. 'I don't know what I think.'

'I think you need help.' His dark eyes grew darker, seemed to expand. 'You've done an amazing job raising our son, but Sam needs a father, especially now he's older.'

10

Maybe Sam did need a father. He and Matt seemed to share a rapport, to connect in a way that blew her away.

Jenny pulled her house key from her pocket and inserted it into the lock of her front door. She and Matt could have gone around the back to the door that was never locked, but she didn't want Matt to know about that door, didn't want him to think he could come in at any time.

'Is he home yet?' Matt asked, his breath fluttering her hair as he stood close behind.

'Sam,' she called.

Music suddenly boomed from Sam's bedroom upstairs and crashed through the ceiling into their ears.

'He's home,' Jenny said. She could feel the tension in her throat, and it was starting to spread to the rest of her body. She started down the hall toward the stairs.

'Wait a minute,' Matt said. 'What's your plan?'

'I don't have a plan.' She kept on walking.

He caught her up. 'You need a plan. Let me talk to him.'

'No.'

'Yes.' Matt touched her arm, his fingers tingling when they met her skin, and her scent was as clear as the stars outside. 'Yes,' he said again. 'I'll go get him.' He ran his hand down her arm and ended at her hand, giving it a gentle squeeze.

She sucked in a breath, her blue eyes smoky-dark.

'Why not make some hot chocolate or whatever Sam likes and I'll bring him down to drink it,' Matt suggested. 'Then we'll talk to him together.'

For a moment he thought she would protest again, but she swiped her eyes and gave a swift nod.

He started up the stairs, his hand on

the railing, his fingers warmed by the smooth polished wood. The house wasn't fancy, was inexpensively decorated, but everywhere he detected Jenny's touch.

She had done a lot with very little, and without any help from him.

Something else he intended to rectify.

At the top of the landing he paused and listened, directing his gaze to the closed door before him. The music was louder now. He would have to knock, but no sound of knuckles could penetrate that din.

Matt stifled a grin. When he was a teen, he'd played the radio just as loudly, could remember his mother shouting at him to turn it down. If the color and shape of the boy's eyes wasn't already a sign, the way he liked his music showed Sam was his son.

Matt knocked on the door. No answer from within. He knocked a little louder then turned the knob.

Sam lay sprawled across his bed

reading a baseball magazine and had wires dangling from buds in his ears.

What the hell?

The kid was listening to something else entirely than the music pounding from the speakers next to his bed.

Posters covered every inch of Sam's walls: baseball players swinging and basketball stars dunking. No football, Matt noticed, although that didn't necessarily preclude an interest in the sport. The boy's small stature would make it tough for him to find success in most of the positions on a football team. Except maybe quarterback if he had any speed.

Matt shook his head. Football was the last thing Jenny would want for her son. She would no doubt give him hell if he even brought it up.

He nudged Sam on the foot. 'Hey kid,' he said.

Sam glanced up from the page he was pretending to read, but made no attempt to pull the wires from his ears.

Matt nodded toward the stereo.

Slowly Sam reached and flicked the off switch. The sudden silence deafened.

How could a kid so young manage not to blink, or look uncomfortable in any way? The boy knew his mom had seen him throw the rock. Why didn't he feel the need to explain?

You had to give the kid credit for nerve.

Matt studied Sam's face and saw features like his own, but in the curve of his lips, he saw traces of Jenny. 'Had a good evening?' Matt asked.

The boy shrugged.

'You're mom's making hot chocolate. She wants you to come down.'

Sam gave his head a barely perceptible shake.

Matt fought an inclination to hug the boy. 'She wants to talk to you,' he said instead.

The boy shook his head a second time, and dropped his gaze back to the magazine.

'I want to talk to you, too,' Matt went on.

166

'I'm tired,' Sam said. 'I'm going to bed.'

'It'll only take a minute.'

The boy looked up. 'I'm not coming down.'

'Then we'll talk here.'

Sam frowned and turned his head away.

Two could play the silent game. Matt glanced around the room and caught sight of a trophy standing on Sam's dresser. He picked it up and read aloud the inscription, 'Most Improved Player, Midget Little League.' He glanced at Sam. 'Way to go, kid.'

The boy's cheeks reddened, but he kept his gaze resolutely on his magazine. 'It doesn't mean anything.'

'You must have worked hard, got better than you were.'

'I still suck,' Sam muttered. His flush swept down to include his neck.

'The coaches must have seen how hard you worked, how much your game changed.'

'Everyone got something.'

'Not everyone got most improved,' Matt said quietly.

Sam glanced up swiftly, then just as swiftly looked away. 'Maybe,' he muttered.

Matt sat down on the foot of his bed. 'So you like baseball?'

'Yeah.'

'What position do you play?'

Sam turned on his side, away from Matt. 'Left field mostly.'

'Impressive,' Matt said. 'You have to be a fast runner to play left field.'

Sam turned back. 'I would rather pitch.'

'Have you told your coach that?'

Sam scowled. 'The coach's son is the pitcher.'

'A team needs more than one.'

The boy shrugged. 'It doesn't matter anyway. Baseball season's over.'

'You could practice for next year.'

Sam shook his head. 'I doubt I'll play next year.'

'Why wouldn't you play?'

'I've got other things to do.'

Matt frowned. 'Other sports, you mean?' Maybe there was room for football yet. Or golf. Golf was good. No knee injuries in golf. He'd enjoy doing a round with Sam, might even show him how to birdy the Fair Winds' seventh hole.

'Not sports,' Sam said firmly.

'What then?'

The boy shrugged. 'Just hanging out.'

'Like you were doing tonight?'

Sam's gaze flickered sideways. 'Who says I was hanging out?'

'Your mom and I saw you.'

Sam sat up in bed. 'I don't know what you mean.'

'You and your buddies were down on McLean Avenue,' Matt said sternly. 'You threw a rock.'

Sam drew up his feet and hugged his legs to him.

'I thought we were going to talk to Sam together.'

Matt swung around at the sound of Jenny's voice. 'We were. We can now.'

'I'm tired,' Sam muttered. 'I don't want to talk.'

Jenny placed her hands on her hips. 'This won't wait.' She shot a look at Matt. 'I've made some hot chocolate. Help yourself.'

'Jenny — ' Matt began.

Sam interrupted. 'I want Matt to stay.'

'Mr. Chambers,' his mother corrected firmly.

'He said, call me Matt,' Sam protested.

'Matt is just fine,' Matt put in hurriedly.

'Matt's staying,' Sam insisted.

He shouldn't feel so damned pleased the boy wanted him there, for it was obvious he just wanted to deflect his mother's wrath. But one glance at Jenny and Matt regretted his delight. She looked exhausted and worried too. Had shadows beneath her eyes that hadn't been there before.

'I'll go,' Matt offered, standing.

Jenny threw him a grateful look.

'No,' Sam cried.

Jenny turned to her son. 'We need to talk. Alone.'

Sam pressed his lips tight, again motioned Matt to stay.

'You went out when you got home,' his mother accused.

Sam threw his magazine towards a pile already on the floor then picked up another one and started to read the cover.

'Look at me, Sam,' Jenny demanded.

He glanced up. 'I don't see what the big deal is. I finished my report.'

'You were supposed to go to bed.'

'It wasn't late.'

'It was late enough.' Jenny gestured at the clock on Sam's bedside table. 'It's ten-thirty already.'

'I'm up this late lots of nights.'

'Not when you've got school in the morning. Not when I expected you to be in bed when I got back.'

The boy's chin jutted out. 'You didn't tell me to be in bed.'

'It goes without saying,' Jenny said impatiently. 'I shouldn't have to tell you

171

every time, and you knew I wouldn't want you out roaming the streets.'

'I wasn't roaming the streets.'

'What were you doing then?'

'Hanging out.' He threw the magazine in his hand onto the floor also. 'With friends,' he added.

'You haven't played with those boys since second grade.'

'Played? I wasn't playing. Playing's for kids.'

Matt touched Jenny's arm. Her cheeks had turned pink again, and there was fire in her eyes. She had to hold back and let her son talk.

Jenny shook off Matt's hand.

'How come you threw the rock?' Matt asked swiftly.

'What rock?' Sam asked, but his eyes flickered left.

'You know which rock.' His mother's voice was stern, but the sorrow in her eyes caught Matt's heart. 'The one that broke Mr. Silverman's lamp.'

Sam's brows drew together. 'I didn't — '

'Didn't what?'

'Mean to,' Sam finished.

'What did you mean to do?' Matt asked softly.

'I don't know. I just . . . '

Jenny's shoulders squared. 'Were you aiming at me?'

'No,' Sam said hotly. 'I wouldn't.' He frowned. 'I didn't mean — '

Jenny moved closer and sat on the bed next to him. 'You almost hit me,' she said softly. 'Almost hit Matt too.'

Sam glared at Matt, then at Jenny. 'You were kissing,' he accused.

'We weren't — ' Jenny began.

'We were,' Matt finished. He might not this minute tell Sam he was his son, but he wasn't going to lie about kissing Jenny. Not when he could still taste her on his lips.

Besides, the boy wasn't stupid. He knew what he had seen and no amount of explaining would erase that image.

Jenny turned to Matt, her blue eyes stricken, and the pink on her cheeks deepening to red.

'I was thanking your mother for a lovely evening,' Matt went on.

Sam's eyebrows met above his eyes. 'You didn't have to kiss her.'

'It's what adults do.'

'Not my mother,' Sam said.

'I'm sure she kisses people all the time.'

'Not men,' Sam muttered. 'Not like that.'

Matt turned to the bookcase to the right of the door, picked up a book and examined its cover. 'We're old friends.'

'You said you were on a date.'

'Sam!' Jenny cried.

'Well, you did.' Sam's chin jutted out and his eyes were stormy.

'Nothing wrong with a date.' Matt glanced toward Jenny. 'I might ask your mom out again tomorrow.'

'Matt!' Jenny protested.

'Dinner?' he suggested. 'And a movie, perhaps? Sam could come along if he would like.'

'What movie?' Sam asked.

'Your choice,' Matt answered.

174

'There'll be no movie,' Jenny said sharply. 'You both seem to have forgotten what we're talking about.'

'Kissing?' Matt asked.

'Throwing rocks,' Jenny snapped. She turned to her son. 'I can't believe you did that, Sam, whatever the reason.'

Sam dropped his gaze and picked at a loose thread at the edge of his quilt. 'I didn't mean to, Mom.'

'What were you thinking?'

'I don't know,' he said, his voice low. 'But I wasn't trying to hit you. If I'd wanted to hit you, I could have done it easy.' He glanced up then and flashed his mother a grin. 'I'm a really good shot.'

'So you meant to hit the lamp.'

'I . . . I guess so,' he admitted. His smile dissolved. 'I just wanted you to stop kissing.'

Matt wanted to go over and hug the boy, wanted to erase the misery from his voice. 'I broke a window once, a basement window.' He had done what boys do when facing a situation. They do whatever comes into their minds or, as in Sam's case, into their hands. There's no thinking, no planning, just a simple burst of adrenalin and action, the whole thing over before you even knew it had begun.

Sam swiped what looked like tears from his eyes. 'Why did you break the window?'

'I didn't make the freshman football squad.' He had felt as though he had to kick something, hadn't counted on his toe hitting the grass first and sending the football in the wrong direction. 'My mother wanted to skin me alive.'

Sam glanced at Jenny.

'She made me do chores for over a month,' Matt continued.

The boy groaned.

'But the next day the coach for the senior team told me I had potential and that I could probably make the sophomore team the following year if I practiced hard enough.' Matt swore then and there to make that team, had turned all his anger into hard work.

Coach Ramsey had helped him.

'So what can you do to fix this, Sam?' Matt asked gruffly.

His son looked up, his dark eyes troubled. 'I could apologize,' he said, 'could offer to pay.'

Matt nodded. 'Might work. Do you have any money?'

'No.' The boy's shoulders slumped. 'I didn't get my allowance this week.'

'Why not?'

'Mom said I hadn't cleaned up my room properly.'

Matt looked around and grinned. 'I can see what she means.'

'It's no laughing matter,' Jenny broke in.

'Not laughing.' Matt turned back to Sam. 'How about you start with your room after school tomorrow, and see if you can earn your allowance.'

'It won't be enough,' Sam said worriedly.

'You can work on getting more later, after you head over to Mr. Silverman's and tell him what happened.'

'I have to tell him I broke his lamp?'

Matt wanted to relent when he heard the regret in the boy's voice, but Sam would learn nothing if he took the easy road. 'You'll feel better once you tell him,' he said, meaning it.

'I doubt it,' Sam said. Then he squared his shoulders. 'All right,' he agreed.

'And after you've apologized you can ask him how much it costs to repair it,' Matt went on.

'I know how much it costs.' Sam's voice was doleful. 'I helped pick those lamps out. It's way more than I've got.'

'Then you'll need a job.'

'A job?' his mother said.

'Nothing that'll interfere with school,' Matt went on. 'But I've got a few things that need doing.'

'Like what?' Jenny asked. 'You don't even live in Seattle anymore.'

'My car needs washing.'

'The Chieftain,' Sam said eagerly.

'Yes,' Matt said. 'It's been in storage for years. Needs a good clean out.'

'It's a cool car,' Sam said excitedly.

'It's a beauty,' Matt agreed. 'But it needs some work.'

'And you want me to help?' Sam's eyes now sparkled with enthusiasm.

'Wash it down, polish it up and help me tune it.'

'Sam doesn't know anything about tuning cars,' Jenny said dubiously.

'Time he learned,' Matt replied.

'Please, Mom,' Sam begged, casting his mother a beseeching look.

Jenny looked at Sam for a long moment then turned back to Matt. 'This seems more like a treat than a job.'

'All the best jobs are treats.' Matt smiled again then turned to Sam and saw him smiling too. Matt held out his hand. 'So it's a deal?'

'Deal,' his son said, putting his smaller hand in his.

11

'Hey, guys, almost done?' Jenny called to Matt and Sam.

Matt nodded and leaned against the Chieftain, wash rag in one hand, scrub brush in the other. Then Sam said something and Matt turned to listen. He wore khakis this morning, cut off at the knees, from which emerged tanned muscular legs. His knees might be damaged, but you couldn't tell just by looking.

He looked good, too good. A familiar tingle shot through Jenny, causing a heat to spread across her face.

The sun, she decided firmly. It was beating down in the best Indian summer fashion and still packed a punch despite the cooler mornings. By noon most days it was hot. It had to be almost noon. Jenny glanced at the watch on her wrist. Sam had given it to her when he was only eight. He had saved his allowance and bought it on the trip they had taken to Disneyland.

Pluto's tail was a little wobbly as it traveled the circle, but wobbly or not, the watch still kept time. Fun time, Sam used to call it.

He hadn't called it fun time in ages.

He was having fun today.

Anxiety pushed aside the heat. In a moment of weakness she'd agreed with Matt's plan, had said that he could spend time with her son. But that was a week ago, on a moon-lit night, when the stars in the sky had befuddled her brain.

There were no stars today, only hot sun, and no whisper of Matt's lips on her cheek. She could see clearly, and what she saw scared her. Her son, her boy, was looking up at Matt and smiling.

He hadn't smiled at her like that in a very long time, had stopped smiling the day Jake said he was marrying Mel. The great thing was since Matt had come into their lives, was that Sam hadn't again asked who his father was. Slowly, thoughtfully, Jenny moved down the steps, and made her way toward the car.

'I've made some sandwiches,' she said, stepping around a bucket filled with soapy water.

'I'm not hungry,' Sam replied. He crouched low to swipe a streak of dirt off the hubcap.

'You haven't eaten since breakfast.'

Although at breakfast Sam had wolfed down eggs, bacon and toast, had eaten as though he'd been surviving on bread and water. He had got up early and was downstairs by seven, had been out on the porch when Matt arrived at eight.

For once she hadn't needed to prompt him to get dressed or wash his face or brush his teeth. He would probably even have cleaned his room again if she'd told him he couldn't work with Matt until it was done. Despite her fears of his growing relationship with

Matt, she didn't want to push the smile from her son's face. Just seeing him happy made her happy too.

'You smell like cookies,' Matt said, as she drew closer. 'I haven't smelled homemade cookies in years.'

She laughed. 'You poor thing.'

He leaned closer and inhaled another breath. 'Cinnamon,' he proclaimed.

'In the cookies,' she concurred.

'And . . . jasmine,' he declared.

'You smell like gasoline.' Although combined with warm water, that scent on Matt was intoxicating. It made her want to kiss him. She suddenly knew that if Sam wasn't there, she probably would have.

Thirteen years before she'd given into the same impulse and had been paying for that impulse every day since then.

She didn't regret Sam, could never regret her son, but sometimes she wished that things had been different, that she could have given her boy a father as he deserved.

She took a step away. 'There's lemonade also.'

'Freshly squeezed?' Matt asked, with a twinkle in his eye.

'Frozen,' she replied, sticking out her tongue. 'You're not in Florida now.'

'You'll have to come out there, if only for the juices.'

'I don't think I'll be going to Florida any time soon.'

'You never know.' He moved closer.

Now he was definitely crowding her space.

Inexplicably her son straightened and trotted toward the house. 'Phone,' Sam called out over his shoulder.

She hadn't heard it ring, although that didn't mean it hadn't. There was some sort of ringing going on inside her head. Added to which was the music in her soul urging her to close the gap to Matt.

She couldn't, shouldn't, didn't dare. Yet suddenly, her hand lifted and touched his shirt. 'You're wet,' she said numbly.

'Sam sprayed me,' he replied.

'He says he's a good shot.' She swallowed hard. 'You should get changed. You must be cold.'

'Sun's warm.' Then his hand covered hers and pressed it to his chest. 'Like you,' he added, pulling her close.

'Don't you dare,' she said.

'Dare what?' he asked.

'Kiss me again.'

His gaze dropped to her mouth. 'What makes you think I'm going to kiss you?'

'Weren't you?' She needed air, couldn't seem to keep her gaze off his lips.

'Maybe,' he murmured.

'Well don't,' she ordered breathlessly.

'Why not?'

'Sam.'

Matt smiled a slow smile. 'We've crossed that hurdle. He's already seen us kiss.'

'And threw a rock because of it.'

'Then he needs to get used to the sight of us kissing.' Matt leaned in

185

closer, their bodies not touching, but an electrical current surged between them.

She would have protested if she could, but she'd already been imagining the touch of his lips. Now she felt the soft fullness of his mouth and tasted the satin smoothness of his lips. Soft became hard as she felt the driving force of the man overtake her.

She wanted to be overtaken. It had been so long. And with no one else, had it ever been as with Matt. Heat, explosions, and surges of strength, and beneath it all, that blossoming of trust.

She had trusted him once.

Did she dare trust him now? She knew she didn't trust herself. Jenny drew away, released the whisper of his touch. 'I should go in.'

Before she could stop him, he kissed her again. This time his kiss promised more to come.

'Matt!' she said, barely able to breathe.

'Don't talk,' he murmured back, his

mouth demanding other things from hers.

God help her, she responded. She even rose on her toes to make herself taller, and met Matt's hunger with hunger of her own. Her senses reeling, she wrapped her arm around his neck and with parted lips took him in.

Then, with a suddenness that stunned, he pulled away. 'What was that you said about sandwiches?' he asked.

'You're hungry?'

'For you.' He brushed a kiss on her cheek. 'But you're right. This is too public. We can't do this here.'

She had worried all week about Matt seeing Sam. She should have worried instead about her own burgeoning feelings, and how on earth she was going to control them.

'Lunch then,' she whispered.

'Sandwiches,' he agreed, smiling with his eyes, 'and after that, dessert.' He drew a finger down her cheek. 'That would be *you*.'

* * *

Thank God Sam had suggested they all go for a swim. From what Matt remembered, the lake was always icy. He needed icy to cool down his body, couldn't seem to be around Jenny without wanting her. He looked towards the water where Sam waited. 'Go deep,' he hollered, then pulled back his arm and threw the football.

He'd told Jenny he wanted to spend time with Sam, but he'd figured out it wasn't enough. He wanted to tell Sam who he really was, and lay claim to the boy as was a father's right.

He also wanted to get closer to Jenny.

But he couldn't break his promise, not after everything that had happened before. The only option he had left was to make Jenny change her mind.

For she must know as well as he that the magic between them had never died. Despite how he'd felt when Coach told him about Jenny and the betrayal that seemed confirmed when he found Jenny in Phil's arms, he now knew that she'd felt equally betrayed when he had left believing she had lied.

He'd been a fool. No matter what he'd been told or what he believed, he should have stayed and worked for the privilege of calling Jenny and Sam family.

He stepped back as Sam threw the ball back to him, overreaching the mark the boy had set. Then Sam raised one arm and Matt threw the ball back, watched as it spiraled through the air. Sam leaped skyward and snagged it mid-jump, then fell backward into the water. For a moment the boy disappeared from view before re-emerging laughing, the ball held aloft.

'Good catch!' Matt called, a lump forming in his throat. How had he filled in his time before this? How would he fill it in again if he didn't have Sam?

Or Jenny?

He glanced to where she sat on a blanket. He'd lost them both once and it was his own damned fault. He wasn't about to lose them again.

* * *

Damn Matt Chambers. He was doing it again. Was making her want what she couldn't have. She'd thought she could live with the proposition he'd offered, could give him access to her son.

But she couldn't. Not without risk. To Sam, to herself . . . most of all, to herself.

She couldn't fall back in love with Matt, for if she did, she would drag her son with her. If what she felt for Matt again ended in disaster, it wouldn't only be *her* heart broken this time.

Sam was already bonding with Matt, hadn't looked so happy in weeks; so warm, so open, so unlike the sullen stranger he'd been growing into lately.

And Matt didn't appear to find parenthood onerous. Rather, he seemed to thrive with every minute spent in Sam's company.

Matt came towards her now, water from the lake dripping off his chest. She was unable to look away from his tanned, muscular body as he dropped to the blanket next to her.

'Time to go?' she asked.

'Sam's still in the water.'

It had been Matt and Sam who had gone in swimming, but it was Jenny who felt the shiver run down her arms.

'Are you cold?' Matt asked.

'A little.' She couldn't reveal that it was him who made her shiver, or how alive her senses were whenever he came near.

He put his arm around her and his cool skin transferred a heat-filled message. She shrugged his arm off, fearing to get burned. 'It's getting late. One of Sam's friends has invited him to his birthday party. We should get going. Sam's due there shortly.'

'Great,' Matt said, picking up a towel and patting himself dry. 'If Sam's going out, you and I can go out too. I'll take you to dinner.'

She shook her head. 'I don't want any dinner. I don't feel very well.'

He placed his palm against her forehead for a second and frowned. 'You are a little hot.'

His touch didn't make her feel any cooler. 'I think I've just had too much sun.' She ran her tongue over dry lips. 'I just need an early night.'

'I'll take Sam to his party.'

'No need to do that.'

'It's no trouble.'

'That's not the point.' She struggled to put her feelings into words. 'You're getting too involved in Sam's life.'

'I thought that was the point.'

'I don't want Sam hurt when you leave.'

Matt touched her hand. 'I'm not going anywhere.'

She glanced toward the water and saw that Sam was now swimming toward the raft offshore.

Matt's gaze followed hers. 'It's time we told him.'

'We agreed you wouldn't say anything yet.'

'Then when?'

She avoided his eyes. 'I don't know. Just not now.'

'Tonight?'

'Not tonight. He'll be at his friend's party.'

'I'll drive him to the party,' Matt said firmly, 'and when he gets back, we'll tell him then.'

Somehow Matt did something to her resolve, exerted some chemistry that made her want to do what he wanted, almost made her believe telling Sam would be all right. Which is why it would be best they not talk in the house. He could convince her of anything when they were alone.

'Let's do as you suggested,' she said briskly. 'Let's go out to dinner.' Neutral ground was what was needed. Maybe in a place full of strangers, doing all the things normal people did, she wouldn't feel the draw of Matt's charm and agree to things she would regret.

'Right,' Matt said, looking pleased. 'I'll pick you both up at six.'

12

Sam no longer seemed bothered by the idea of her and Matt going out, for he leaned forward from the back seat and poked his head between them. 'Can you come in to Nick's house for a minute, Matt?'

'Sure,' Matt agreed, shooting a glance at Jenny.

Jenny frowned and tried to decipher what was going on in her son's head. He'd known his friend Nick his entire life, and had never been shy about going to his house. Why this sudden desire to have Matt come in with him, and why wasn't he asking her to accompany him also? 'Are you all right?' she asked her son.

'I'm fine,' he replied.

'Why do you want Matt to go into Nick's with you?'

Sam glanced at Matt, then back at

her. 'I sort of promised the guys . . . '

'Promised them what?'

'That they could meet Matt.'

Jenny blinked. She should have realized Matt's big football star status would make him a hero in Sam's friends' eyes also.

'I'll be glad to meet your friends,' Matt said, looking pleased. 'If they want we could meet up tomorrow as well, maybe throw the football around a little.'

'That would be awesome!' Sam agreed, his eyes lighting up at the suggestion.

They pulled up at the curb in front of Nick's house, and Sam hurried from the car and bounded up the stairs. Matt followed more slowly and then the door shut behind them and Jenny was alone.

It was maybe five minutes that Matt stayed inside, but it felt much longer than that to Jenny. When he left, Sam and his friends crowded around him to say goodbye, an athletic Pied Piper mesmerizing the kids. If he stayed in

Seattle any longer, he'd be in danger of taking over the entire city.

Finally, Matt returned, and climbed in behind the wheel. He glanced in her direction and his eyebrows knotted. 'Are you all right?'

'I'm fine.'

This time he touched her cheek rather than her forehead, but pronounced, 'You're still hot. I'm taking you home.'

'No!' She forced a smile. 'I need food, that's all. I get cranky when I'm hungry.'

With a last swift scrutiny, he turned the key in the ignition, shifted the car into drive and pulled away from the curb. Silence drifted around them for a long moment.

'Where are we going?' Jenny finally asked.

'Downtown,' Matt answered. 'There's a seafood restaurant near Pike's Market. I don't know if it's still there, but it used to be good.'

'It's still there.' She glanced down at

her short cotton dress. 'If I'd known we were going there, I'd have worn something different.'

'You look wonderful,' he replied.

★ ★ ★

He made her feel wonderful, and that's just what she couldn't allow. She twirled her fork through her seafood fettuccine, but didn't feel like eating any more.

Matt stared at the uneaten portion on her plate. 'You're not eating,' he said, stating the obvious. 'Are you still feeling unwell?'

'Just not as hungry as I thought, I guess.'

'We'll get the waitress to pack up the rest. You can take a doggy bag home for your cat.'

'Twister will think he's died and gone to heaven. He's not used to eating such rich food.'

'Salmon fettuccini is not that rich.'

'Our leftovers don't usually come

from fancy restaurants.'

'We can change all that.' He motioned to the waitress to bring their bill.

'What do you mean?'

'I haven't given you a cent for Sam all these years. That's going to change.'

'I don't want your money.' She grabbed her purse from where it hung on her chair and dug inside for some cash.

Matt waved her hand away when she tried to pass it to him. 'I owe this to you both,' he said gruffly.

'You just want to feel better.'

'I do,' he said simply, 'but it will take a lot more than that.'

She gritted her teeth. 'Sam and I might not live in a fancy house, but he has everything he needs.'

He touched her hand across the table. 'Not everything.'

'You can't buy your way into being a father.'

'I'm offering more than money.'

'And you can't just be thinking about what *you* want.' She regretted her words as soon as they were spoken when she saw the hurt flit through his eyes. 'Let's dance,' she said, then regretted that too. She didn't want to talk, also didn't want to dance, for when they danced, their bodies would be close. At Jake's wedding, she'd sworn she'd never dance with him again, for the sensations flowing between them had been lightning hot.

'Good idea,' Matt said, taking her hand. Within seconds she was up and in his arms.

On the dance floor they swiftly found the beat of the rumba. 'Who taught you to dance?' Jenny gasped, losing her breath as he twirled her through a tricky sequence of steps. He then drew her so close she could hear the beating of his heart, could feel his body's rhythm call to her own.

'Jenny — '

She was caught in the magic of the moment. His arms tightened around her as though they were lovers . . . in love . . . in sync, as they had been in the beginning.

But she wasn't a teenager anymore. She couldn't think the word love, could certainly not say it. She pulled away, felt the drag of his embrace. 'We should go,' she said numbly.

'I want to stay here, want to hold you in my arms.'

She wanted that too, but couldn't give in to that want. There was too much at stake to make decisions based on emotion. She swallowed hard. 'It's almost time to pick up Sam.'

'The party's not over for at least another hour.' Matt dropped feather kisses across her cheek. 'Nick's mother said she'd drop Sam off.'

'Nevertheless.'

He pulled away and gazed into her eyes, making her tremble with pent-up desire. He was starting to feel again the other half to her whole.

'You're right,' he said. 'Let's get out of here.'

★ ★ ★

Being in the car was no less intimate than circling the dance floor in Matt's embrace. It was now getting dark and despite the Chieftain's size, the front seat didn't give her much distance from Matt.

It would take more than the width of one adult body when the space of a continent hadn't been enough. He'd lived in Florida for the last thirteen years, but she still remembered his touch on her skin, still sensed his spirit circling her thoughts.

She felt suddenly drained. She didn't want him to go, couldn't bear that he stay. She sucked in a breath, tried to draw it down deep, tried to take from it the strength she needed. Then she realized he'd missed the turn-off to her house. 'Where are we going?' she demanded.

'To the beach,' he replied. 'We haven't been there together in years.'

'It's after dark. We won't be able to see a thing.'

'That's the point,' he explained. 'No

distractions, no children, no excuses not to talk.'

'I don't recall talking the last time we were there.'

'We were busy,' he agreed.

They'd been busy making love.

'We can't relive the past,' she whispered.

He turned down a paved road that grew into gravel the closer they got to the beach front parking lot. 'The past was where everything began.' He didn't look at her as he spoke, simply drove until he came to where the road ended. 'We have to deal with what went wrong between us, then somehow find a way to make things right.'

If they'd still been kids, the night would have been perfect with its solitude, the warm air, the joy of being together.

But they weren't kids anymore and they weren't together.

He turned off the ignition and turned to face her. 'This was where we first kissed.'

'I'm surprised you remember.'

'I remember everything about that time. How young we were, how beautiful you were.' He raised his hand and stroked her face. 'You're still so beautiful.'

She shouldn't want him to touch her and tried to twist away, but found to her dismay that she couldn't.

'I've missed you, Jenny,' he said softly.

'I've missed you too.'

'I thought we'd never have a chance to be together again.' His eyes darkened to a shade deeper than the black night and his hand on her cheek dropped to her shoulder. He pulled her close, covering her mouth with his.

He couldn't taste this good. Not in real life. She'd thought what she remembered had been mere fantasy, but his lips were tinged with the brush of fine wine and the fire of his hand seemed to burn her skin. Her lips parted and his tongue found its way inside.

'Matt,' she breathed, her tongue

203

curling around his.

'I want you, Jenny.'

In answer, she raised her arms, wrapped them around his neck and shifted sideways in her seat. To where she could touch him and be touched by him.

'Remember this?' He kissed her more deeply, taking her breath and turning her soul inside out.

'I remember,' she said. She had never forgotten, no matter how much she tried. But his kisses felt different than before; stronger, more mature, more wildly sexual.

He ran his fingers through her hair, untangling her curls and gently lifting its silky smoothness from her neck. It felt good to have it gone, to give air to her heat.

She'd been afraid to get close, but now wanted him nearer. He swept his hand down and around her shoulders, pulling her closer with every motion. Then he slipped his hand inside the top of her dress and touched her breast with a lover's touch. He undid the buttons one by one, opening her dress from the top to its hem.

Exposing her skin.

Filling her with need.

She met his desire with passion of her own and was stunned by the sensations, by the melting of limbs and heightened awareness.

A tingling began deep in her belly and spiraled upward until it reached her chest. She strained toward Matt, felt his answering response.

Somehow she breathed, smelled his scent as she did so, the fresh mint smell of soap and shampoo. It was different from the old days when he'd played football, when the sweat of his body had mingled with grass. She'd liked that smell too, had also liked how he looked, all hot and flushed and breathing hard.

'Matt,' she moaned, and writhed closer to him, not wanting him to stop, simply wanting his touch.

She wanted him, needed him, had

desired him for years, and now she wanted only to feel all he could give. She glanced over his shoulder and saw nothing but darkness and mist-covered glass. The windows of his car were steamed from their heat, but the heat inside was greater than without.

'Matt,' she whispered, his name slipping from her lips easily, contrasting sharply to the hard body lying against hers. A body now aligned with her curves.

Energy hung in the air between them, then like lightning, shafted toward the earth. She strained toward Matt. There was no crying halt, no point of return.

He ignited. She inflamed. They both gave and received. Yesterday, today, it no longer mattered. Only this moment in time made sense. A moment Jenny wished could last forever. A moment, when it came, that left her spent.

'I don't think I'm breathing,' she said, at last, sighing.

'I know I'm not,' Matt whispered in her ear.

Jenny kissed his chin. 'It doesn't seem to matter.'

'Give it time.'

He gazed at her with light-filled eyes, eyes she again believed she could trust. He kissed her cheek. 'Let's go back to your place. Sam will be home soon.'

Sam. Her son. The son of this man.

For a segment of time, she'd put that knowledge from her, had escaped to a spot where she didn't have to think. Now she must pull the knowledge back and make decisions that could change her life.

13

Matt's hand touched her back as they entered her front door and lingered there as though it belonged.

She wanted him to belong, had always wanted that, but now there was more than her feelings at stake. She had to think of Sam and what was best for him.

She swept into the kitchen, motioning Matt to follow. 'Coffee?' she offered. The questions in her brain threatened to overwhelm. She turned on the radio, tried for normalcy instead, deciding the news would jar her back into the real world.

'No coffee,' Matt replied. Then he touched her again, only her arm, but it tilted her world, even here and now, in the middle of her familiar things.

He came up behind her and touched her neck.

She shivered and longed to lean back against him.

'Things have changed between us,' he murmured in her ear.

She turned to face him. 'Tell me what's changed.' She needed him to say the words that would heal the past.

'We just made love.'

Her throat grew dry. It had been wonderful, but the last time they'd made love, he'd gone away.

The music on the radio died, and in its place came the ringing tone that signaled the start of the hour's weather report.

'*Batten down the hatches, Seattle,*' the weather man said cheerily. '*There's a bad storm coming in from the Northwest.*'

'I need you and Sam,' Matt went on, raising his voice over the radio announcer. 'If I had believed you, things would have been so different.' Pain flitted through his eyes. 'When I thought you lied, I couldn't stand it. I'd already been through that with my father.'

Jenny's heart constricted. 'What happened with your father?'

Matt sucked in a breath. 'He lied to my mother, my sisters and me.'

'How did he do that?'

'He told us he'd been offered a job in Texas, said he'd go there first and then send for us.'

'And he didn't?' she asked.

'No.' The single word came out strangled. 'He'd made promises before that he never kept. We should have known better than to think he'd keep this one.' Matt exhaled a long breath. 'My mother had to raise three kids on her own. Money was tight, pretty much non-existent. I got a job as soon as I was old enough and tried to help my mom provide for the family.'

'You were just a kid.'

Matt turned his head and stared out of the window, seemed to gaze unseeingly at the steadily darkening sky.

'What about your dad?'

Matt turned back to face her. 'He didn't even write. It was as though he dropped off the face of the planet.'

'What happened to him?'

'God knows. My dad was a drunk. We don't even know if there ever was a job.' Matt's brows drew in and he looked at Jenny with an expression so fierce she took a step back. 'I don't want Sam thinking I chose anything over him.'

She touched Matt's shoulder, wanting to take him into her arms. 'Drinking too much is an illness,' she said gently.

'Lying is not.'

'Sometimes you lie to protect the people you love. Maybe your father did it for that reason. Maybe Coach did too.'

Matt's lips twisted. 'I thought Coach was different. But this isn't about Coach or my father. This is about you and me and the baby we created.'

Old pain surfaced and struck Jenny's heart. She had never wanted the star football player Coach created, had only wanted Matt to have and to hold.

'I should have trusted you,' Matt

went on, touching her now, taking hold of her hand.

Trust was such a small word, yet so big when you tried to hold it.

'And I should have explained,' Jenny replied, 'rather than getting angry and telling you to go.' She touched his cheek. 'We both made mistakes.'

Matt raised her hand, and kissed her palm. 'I'm sorry, Jenny,' he said simply. 'I don't know how I can make up for thirteen years of absence, but I hope you and Sam will let me try.'

'And if you fail?' She couldn't bear it if he failed.

'I won't fail,' he said, his voice certain.

'Bad news for Seahawks fans tonight. Unconfirmed reports say the Miami Dolphins have stolen Seattle's favorite son — offering Matt Chambers a deal he couldn't refuse.'

At the sound of Matt's name, Jenny's attention jerked towards the radio.

'When questioned, Chambers' agent was very tight-lipped, simply stated

there were offers on the table.'

'Matt!' Jenny cried.

'Bloody press,' Matt growled. 'Don't worry Jenny, I'll be there for Sam. I'm his father. I won't let him down.'

'My *father*?'

At the sound of Sam's voice, Matt and Jenny spun around, found Sam in the doorway, his face drained of color. But his eyes were darker than Jenny had ever seen them and were trained on Matt like laser rays.

'You're my father?' he cried. 'How can you be?' Sam turned to Jenny. 'Mom?'

Jenny's heart broke.

'Mom,' he said again, only higher this time.

At times in the past weeks, Sam had seemed to have grown up, but at this moment he was a frightened little boy, looking to her to make things better.

She couldn't make it better. Not when she felt as though she'd been punched in the stomach. 'What Matt says is true.' Her voice had come out even higher than Sam's, and sounded as though it had been squeezed through a tube.

'Why didn't you tell me? Why didn't you marry?' Sam swallowed hard. 'Didn't Matt want me either?'

Behind her, Matt moved, as though to explain, but Sam turned swiftly and ran out the door.

'Sam,' Jenny called, chasing after him.

Matt streaked past her despite his bum knee, but by the time they got to the front porch, there was no longer any sign of Sam.

'He's gone,' Matt said, scanning the street to the right and left.

Jenny pushed past him. 'He can't have gone yet.'

'I don't see him. Do you?'

Jenny strained her eyes to adjust to the darkness, but could see nothing resembling a boy in flight.

'Where would he go?' Matt demanded.

'I don't know,' she said desperately.

The darkness seemed to deepen,

even as they stood, growing black with the gathering clouds of the storm.

Jenny stared at the clouds, fear surging in her heart, then she turned to Matt and clutched his arm. 'We've got to find him,' she said. 'It's going to rain.'

Matt lifted his wrist and glanced at his watch. 'It's not that late. It's just nine o'clock. Don't worry. He'll come back.'

If Sam felt as bad as she, he'd stay away. 'He's upset,' she said, her chest constricting.

'He'll be all right.'

Fear turned Jenny's mouth as dry as ashes. 'You don't understand.' She clenched her fists tight. 'Sam has asthma.'

Matt's eyebrows drew in.

'When he gets upset, he could have an attack.'

'Which means what exactly?' Matt demanded.

'He can't breathe.' Nor could she at this minute. All her air had gone. 'He'll need his medication. He has a puffer.' She pulled in a breath that hurt going down. 'He doesn't have it with him. I saw it on the kitchen counter when we came in. He could get really bad.'

'How bad?' Matt asked, his eyes becoming black holes in his face.

'I've had to take him to the hospital a few times. If I hadn't, he might have died.'

Matt's face turned pale. 'He's not going to die.'

'I just wish we had told him. I wish I'd agreed.' She had never thought she would wish for such a thing. 'I wish he hadn't found out the way he did.'

Matt gripped her shoulders and gave them a little shake, as though to battle the hysteria rising in her chest. 'He's going to be all right,' he said again.

'You don't know — '

'He's tough. He's had to be.'

'He's just a little boy.'

Matt pulled her to him, gave her a swift hug, then separated from her and stared into her eyes.

She felt a connection flow between them, felt sick at the thought of him leaving again. Swiftly, she pushed the thought away.

'Has he ever run away before?' Matt asked.

'Just once, years ago. But this is different.'

'What about friends?' Matt asked grimly. 'Could he have gone to a friend's house?'

'I don't know.' She took a step back, tried to resurrect a brain gone dead. 'We should call the police.'

'We will, but I don't think they'll do anything yet.'

'Why wouldn't they help? Sam's out there alone.'

He moved to pull her to him again.

She took another step back, didn't dare to share his warmth or his strength, not if soon she would be all alone.

Matt frowned, his arms dropping to his sides. 'They'll say if he ran away then he'll come back. And he will,' he said tersely. 'You have to believe that.'

'But he's so young.'

'He's not that young.' Matt's determination shone from his eyes. 'He'll be at a friend's. Now get a pen and paper and write down any numbers you can think of. You can start phoning while I go out and look.'

'I can't sit here phoning. Not while my child's out there in the dark. I'll come with you.'

Matt's expression gentled. 'You need to stay here. Someone has to be here when Sam comes home.'

'And if he doesn't?' Jenny's skin turned clammy.

'He'll get hungry . . . tired . . . no kid goes without food.'

'When he ran away before,' she said, forcing a smile, 'he lived off the land.'

'How old was he then?'

'Seven.'

Matt eyebrows lifted. 'That's a little young for living off the land.'

'He went with his friend Ricky, who was eight. They went to the spare lot next to Ricky's house. They caught ants — ' She shuddered. ' — and dipped them in melted chocolate.'

Matt's lips twitched.

'It's not funny,' she cried. 'Sam said he could have lived off ants for weeks.'

'Yes, but how long did he actually stay away?'

'A couple of hours,' Jenny admitted. 'But it was long enough. Ricky's mother and I were out of our minds with worry.' Jenny's skin grew colder yet. 'And that other time he wasn't angry. He had no reason to stay away longer.' Her throat grew tight. 'Finding out that the man dating your mother is actually your father is enough to traumatize a boy for life!'

Matt pulled in a breath. 'I'm going now. Will you be all right?'

The caring in his eyes nearly did her in. But she'd never be all right. Not if he left. Not if her son was lost in the storm. She turned her head, trying not to cry. She didn't want Matt to go, but didn't want him to stay either. She simply wanted her boy back so she could explain. And when that was done, discover just what Matt intended. Then start the process of trying to forget.

'I'll find him,' Matt promised. 'He can't have gone far. You start the calls.'

'He hasn't had time to get to any of his friends yet.'

'No, but if you call, people will know he's run away and will phone you when he shows up at their house.'

Jenny peered past the Chieftain parked in her drive. 'Maybe he's hiding. He could slip in anywhere.'

'I'll find him, Jenny.' Matt's black eyes met hers. 'Trust me,' he said.

She wanted to trust him when he hadn't told her he intended to take a job three thousand miles away?

'Trust me,' he said again, then opened his arms.

She fought the inclination to fall into his strength. 'Just go,' she said.

★　★　★

'Missing!' Vivian exclaimed.

'Missing,' Jenny said wearily.

'For how long?'

'Not long. Have you or John seen him?'

'No,' Vivian said. 'But we live across town. How would he get to our house?'

'He's pretty resourceful. Can you keep an eye out for him?'

'I'm coming over.'

'No, Viv, you can't. I want you to stay put in case he comes to you.'

'But you need me,' Vivian said.

'Sam may need you more. Besides — ' Her voice broke. 'Matt's here.'

'Matt's there?' Curiosity was palpable in her friend's voice. 'What's he doing there?'

'Well, he's not actually here at the moment. He's out looking for Sam.'

'But he was there? I knew it! You two did hit it off.'

'I don't have time to talk about that now. I've got more calls to make.'

'You don't have to talk,' Vivian said triumphantly. 'I could tell you were both interested by the way you looked at each other.'

'I've got to go,' Jenny said, drained. 'Phone me if you hear from Sam.'

'You phone me when he comes home, and if he's not home by morning, I'm coming over.'

Not home by morning. The idea was unthinkable. Sam had to come home and in the next few minutes. She'd seen the missing child ads on cereal and milk boxes, and appeals from their parents on radio and TV, but she'd never imagined she would be in their spot, waiting for the simple sound of her child's voice.

She couldn't do this much longer, stay in while Matt was out. She had phoned every friend Sam had ever had and not one of them had seen her son.

She'd even phoned the boys who'd been with him the other night, but each one had said they hadn't seen him since then.

What if they were lying? Even worse, what if they weren't?

Where in God's name could Sam be? And where was Matt? He'd been gone for two hours. If he didn't get home soon, she was phoning the police.

It frightened her to think that they needed the police, but if Sam stayed on the street, anything could happen. The world was full of scary people, many of them willing to harm a child.

There came a knock. She raced to the door, but before she could turn the knob, Matt was in.

Her hand reached out of its own volition, wanting to touch him, to clear away the frown furrowing his brow. She pulled it back, willing her heart not to leap at his nearness. 'You look exhausted,' she said instead.

'I'm fine,' he said grimly. 'No word yet?'

'Nothing. Nobody's seen him.'

'I've checked every street in a ten block radius. If he's outside anywhere, I'm sure I would have seen him.'

'We've got to phone the police.'

'I already did.'

'What did they say?'

'That they'll keep their eyes open, but that it's early yet. They expect he'll just come home sooner or later.' Matt's lips tightened. 'I'm going back out.'

'I'm going with you.'

'You need to stay by the phone.'

'I'll take my cell. I can't just wait here. I'm going crazy.' She stopped as she struggled to get more words past the dry place in her mouth. 'And Sam's puffer,' she mumbled. 'I've got to bring that.'

Matt gathered her sweater from the chair on which she'd flung it and carefully, gently placed it around her shoulders. 'Come on then, if you're coming.'

She looked like hell. Her hair was coming free of the elastic that held it and her eyes were two saucers in a pale, pale face. The spark she normally showed had disappeared. Only her chin remained the same, and it was thrust out as if to show the world she wasn't afraid.

But she was afraid. And so was he. If anything happened to Sam it would be his fault. For the thousandth time since Sam whirled away, Matt wished he hadn't pushed as hard as he had. He should have taken things slower, not thought about himself and all the time he had missed with his son. He'd been crazy to think Sam would be happy to discover who his father was, and that his father was back in his life.

He'd often thought of what he would have done, if *his* father had returned. He should have known the kid would rather run a mile than open himself to hurt.

Matt took Jenny's elbow and guided her through the dark to the Chieftain.

Jenny lowered herself into the front seat. 'Where do we look?'

'The bus station,' Matt said, turning the key in the ignition.

'The bus station!' Jenny cried. 'Sam wouldn't go there.'

'He might if he knows anyone who lives out of town. Does he?' Matt turned and searched her eyes. 'Is there someone he might get in touch with? Someone he'd run to?'

'No,' Jenny said. Then her eyes widened. 'Unless, maybe Dan. Dan was Sam's best friend. He moved away a year ago. Sam might go to him.'

'Where does he live?'

'Portland.' She frowned. 'But Sam has no money. He couldn't buy a ticket.'

Matt gripped the wheel. 'I gave him money. To pay him for the work he did on the car. He was going to take it over to Mr. Silverman tomorrow.'

'Even so,' Jenny said stubbornly, 'I can't believe he would just leave.'

'He's hurt. He's not thinking.'

'He knows he's not allowed.'

Matt swung the car out onto the road. 'He's probably not worrying about what he's allowed.'

'The bus station's full of strangers,' Jenny protested.

'Not all strangers are evil.'

Jenny's chest grew tight. 'The sort of

stranger that hangs out in bus stations might be evil.'

'Don't think about that. Let's just get there and check it out.' But he had been doing nothing but thinking for the past two hours as he drove around Jenny's neighborhood looking for Sam. Thinking about how he had left before his son was born, how he hadn't been there to protect him as he grew up. And now when he got the chance to know his son, he'd succeeded only in driving him away.

Matt pressed harder on the gas. He was driving too fast, but needed to go faster, had to get to where his son might be.

His tires sprayed water from the puddles on the roads. The sultry weather from the day had turned into water. From the sky huge black drops smashed against the pavement.

He hoped to God Sam had found shelter, was resting safely at his friend's house in Portland. Matt turned the windshield wipers to a higher speed. If

Portland was where Sam was headed, he wouldn't be there yet. There hadn't been time for a bus to get that far.

If he was even on a bus. What if he tried to hitchhike?

He listened as Jenny again called the police, watched her grim face as she relayed what they said, that most runaways come home within a few hours.

But the police hadn't seen the pain on Sam's face, or the fear in Jenny's eyes when he told her not to worry. Sam would be back — he'd make sure of that — but he didn't think that would happen in a few hours.

After twenty-four hours, he'd officially be a missing person. Twenty-four hours. It was too long.

Jenny's cell rang.

They both jumped at the sudden sound.

'Hello,' Jenny answered, then listened intently. 'It's for you,' she said, shoving the phone at Matt.

'Hello,' Matt said.

'Matt,' Coach answered. 'Glad I caught you. Wasn't sure how long you'd be in town.'

'How did you get this number?'

'I phoned Jake's office a few days ago. Knew your girlfriend worked for him. They gave me her number.'

Matt tightened his one-handed grip on the wheel. 'Go on,' he said, into the cell.

'I . . . wanted to see if everything was all right.' Coach gave a little cough. 'Last time we talked.' He coughed again. 'I've been thinking.' There was a long pause. 'I might have been wrong, how I handled things back then.'

Matt had never before heard Coach say he was sorry, had thought him a man incapable of uttering the word.

'Thought I'd call,' Coach continued, 'to see if there was anything I could do. Maybe talk to your girlie, tell her I made a mistake.'

'Now's not a good time. Her son . . . my son . . . Sam is missing.' Beside him

Jenny wrapped her arms around her body.

'Missing?' Coach repeated.

'Yes. He's run away.' Matt glanced through the windscreen to the driving rain beyond. 'We're looking for him now.'

'Have you called the police?'

'Yes,' Matt replied. 'They say it's too soon for them to get involved. They'll keep an eye out, but they think he'll come back.' Matt tried to keep the tension from his voice, didn't want Jenny to know his fear.

'Then we'll find him ourselves,' Coach said gruffly. 'I'll get the guys, the Junior team too. Where's your kid live? We'll span out from there.'

Coach's offer was better than saying sorry. It showed more than words how the old man felt.

'Thanks,' Matt said, his heart suddenly full. He gave Coach the address then signed off.

'That was Coach,' Matt said, but could see from Jenny's eyes she'd already guessed it. 'He's getting his team together. They're going to look for Sam.'

'Good,' Jenny said, her voice scarcely audible. She straightened her shoulders. 'That will help.'

What helped was that the old man cared. Matt nodded once then stepped on the gas, maneuvering the car past the upper entrance to Pike's Market, then dipping down the hill towards the pier. Might as well take a scan along the shore, and swing past the ball park and the football stadium. No games tonight, but Sam might not know that, might think he could go there and kill some time before coming home and facing his mother.

But there was no sign of a twelve-year-old boy hiking along a rainswept sidewalk. Matt pulled out from behind the car in front, and swerved to the left up a side street. 'To the bus station now,' he said, and almost before he knew it, they were there.

'Park there,' Jenny directed.

Matt pulled into a spot in front of the station, not caring that it was a no-parking zone. A quick in and out was all he intended, a swift scan of the benches to make sure Sam wasn't there, then checking the buses to see if he was on one of them.

He was out the car door almost before they were stopped, and Jenny was right behind him, her hand finding his. He squeezed it hard, glad to be able to touch her again. She'd seemed frozen in her own space since Sam had overheard them. Together they pushed open the door of the building.

Jenny stared around the cavernous room, her spirits dropping to match the ambience of the place. Her son couldn't be here. It was horrible here.

There were too many people, some sitting, some standing, and some sprawling in corners watching with slanting glances. Some had luggage, were actual travelers, while others carried plastic bags. Not filled with food, or items they had purchased, but rather with the precious debris of their lives. It was, apparently, all they had left.

The storm outside must have driven them in from the streets, the park benches, and the alleys, from wherever people slept who had no home or loved ones.

Her son had both, but still he had left.

How could he have come to this place of transition?

Jenny's chest constricted. She didn't want Sam to be here, but she'd rather have him here than not find him at all.

'Shall we split up?' she asked, trying to find the courage to let go of Matt's hand.

'No,' he replied, giving her fingers another squeeze. 'I don't want you wandering around this place alone.'

'Sam's alone.'

He shot her a look, must have seen the fear in her heart. 'We'll find him,' he promised, and pulled her close.

14

The comfort of Matt's embrace shot straight through her and just for a moment Jenny allowed herself to relax. Then she pulled away and gazed into his eyes. 'We've got to hurry. We'll cover more ground alone.'

Thunder clapped outside, making them both jump.

'Check out the ticket booths,' Matt said tersely. 'Ask if anyone has sold Sam a ticket.'

'They might not remember.'

'Let's hope they do. I'll check the buses.'

'Will they let you on to the platform without a ticket?'

Matt's expression was grim. 'I'd like to see them stop me.'

Jenny watched him stride away and felt comforted by his certainty. She wished his hand was still holding hers.

She tried to force the sinking feeling from her heart, tried to keep faith that they would find Sam and get him back home before he was harmed, by the night, the storm, or the people who came across him, a not-so-big boy who was thinking his own thoughts. Not watching as he should for lurking danger.

He had never faced danger, at least not alone. He'd always had her. And now he had Matt.

But did either one of them actually have Matt?

She moved towards where the ticket booths stood, passing as she went an alcove leading to lockers. She'd look there first.

A young man sat on the bench before her, his black gaze darting to her face then away. Was he a traveler or was he sitting there to prey on others, someone like Sam who was vulnerable and alone? Before she could move past him to the locker room, the man looked again in her direction.

'Spare change?' he asked, holding out his hand.

Mutely, she shook her head. She had no money, had come out of the house without her purse.

'Want a drink?' he offered, holding out a bottle.

Again she shook her head, then with sudden decision pulled Sam's picture from her pocket. She held it out. 'Have you seen this boy?'

The man's hand was filthy, but he held the picture carefully at its edge. 'No,' he said finally, and handed it back. 'Your kid?'

'Yes.'

'Runaway?' the man asked gruffly.

She didn't want to admit that Sam had run away, didn't want to think he didn't want to be with her. But a runaway was what he was. She straightened her shoulders and gave a nod.

'Better find him,' the man said, taking a swig from his bottle. 'The world's a big place.'

She had never before realized just how huge. It could swallow her son and never give him back. With shaky legs she stepped around the man's bench and headed to where the lockers wound their way into the alcove.

'Ain't gone that way,' the man called after her. 'I'd have seen him if he had.'

There was no reason she could think of to believe him, except for the sympathy she had glimpsed in the man's eyes.

'Thanks,' she murmured, and hurried back the way she came.

The line at the ticket counter was unbelievably long, probably because most of the counters were closed. Murmuring excuses, Jenny pushed her way to the front.

'Hey,' protested a man she nudged to one side, but one glance at Jenny's face stilled his objections.

'I won't be a minute,' she told him hurriedly, then turned to face the ticket seller behind the wicket. 'I'm looking for my son.' She held up Sam's picture.

A picture she'd taken just last Christmas. In it, Sam's face was wreathed in smiles. He had been thrilled with the present she'd just given him, a new mountain bike in his favorite color, black. She'd been worried back then that he might get injured careering down trails with more verve than skill, but right now she'd give anything to see him riding, head dipped low over the handlebars.

'Lots of kids come through here, lady,' the ticket seller said.

'But he's only twelve. Surely there aren't many boys that age buying tickets?'

'You're right about that. They're more inclined to try to sneak on the bus.'

Sneak on the bus. Jenny's heart turned over. That was a possibility she hadn't considered. She'd imagined every other sort of disaster, but if her child could simply climb on a bus and get miles away before being discovered, what chance had she and Matt of getting him home safely?

She banished the terrifying thought from her head. 'So you haven't seen him?' she persisted.

'Not that I remember.' The woman glanced pointedly over her shoulder to the customer next in line.

Tears threatened to spill down Jenny's cheeks. She swallowed hard and edged her way back through the crowd. She caught sight of Matt striding along the departure platform. Heart in throat, she raced to catch up.

By the time she reached him, he was already at the first bus, talking to the driver and scanning the windows. She scrambled up the steps and peered into the bus's interior.

The vehicle was almost empty. Two elderly ladies sat near the front, their gazes darting nervously toward their luggage, which a handler was throwing with more strength than care into the compartment beneath the bus. A scattering of single men waited patiently for the bus to get moving, but

Jenny couldn't see her boy amongst them.

Then at the back, she saw a group of youths, talking amongst themselves in too-loud voices. She took a step forward but couldn't see Sam hidden between their duffel bags, crouching down to making himself small.

'Got a ticket, ma'am?' a uniformed driver asked, climbing up the steps behind her.

'No,' she replied. 'I'm just looking for my son.' She thrust forward Sam's picture. 'Have you seen him?'

The driver shook his head then stood aside, motioning her back outside the bus.

Matt had already passed on to the next vehicle. She longed to run to him, to receive his reassurance, but there was no time now for comfort. They had to find Sam before he disappeared for good.

She moved to the next bus, and then to the next, overlapping Matt as they hurried about their task. Finally they came to the end of the buses, but despite all her hope, hadn't found her little boy.

Jenny's throat felt so dry, she thought it might crack, yet her tears were now streaming down her face, combining with the rain still descending in sheets.

Sam had run out without a jacket, was wearing his usual flimsy tee shirt. He'd be freezing in this weather if he wasn't some place dry. Even dry, if he was outside, he'd be feeling the cold, for the wind was coming out of the north, the first cold wind that presaged the turning season. A sudden gust swirled up Jenny's legs, lifting her dress and raising goose bumps on her arms.

She shivered and wrapped her arms around her body, tried to draw her thin sweater in more tightly. Then a hand touched her shoulder and Matt swung her around, pulling her in close.

'You're freezing,' he said, drawing his hands down her arms.

'I'm all right,' she replied, but her teeth suddenly chattered.

'You're not all right.' Matt's eyes grew darker than the night itself, but were dark like a cave, a refuge from the storm.

She didn't want to feel the refuge for she feared her hope that what Matt said was true, that he would be there for her and Sam. Yet when she tried to push him away, another emotion flooded in.

It couldn't be love, not here, not now. Not when her world was falling apart.

'Where else?' Matt growled.

His question shook her from the place she had fled, full of hopes and dreams and passions unexplored. There was no time for love, only time for Sam, for figuring out where her boy was.

'I don't know,' she said, shaking her head.

'Friends, bus station — ' Matt ticked off the possibilities they had covered on his fingers. 'What about the train station?'

'Sam wouldn't go there. But then, I didn't think he would come here either.' Jenny took a step back. 'I don't know what to think.'

'I think you should go home.'

'I'm staying with you.'

'You're tired — '

More than tired. She felt as though she hadn't slept in days.

' — freezing.'

Like ice. Only in the places Matt touched, could she feel the difference.

'Sam might be home by now,' Matt suggested.

Hope surged through her then just as swiftly died. 'He won't come home yet. Sam's stubborn,' she said.

'He must get that from you.'

She glanced at Matt, startled, then saw his half smile. She tried to smile back, but the effort at lightness hurt more than worry. 'No stubborn bones in me,' she said, with a sigh.

'So if he wouldn't go home, where would he go?'

Her whole body ached as if from the flu, and her head felt as though it were wrapped in wool. There seemed no way a thought could emerge.

'Hangouts? Hideouts!' Matt suggested. 'All kids have those.'

Not Sam. Not her son. Until the last few months, he'd seemed content at home, had played with his friends in their own back yard, or in the street shooting hockey pucks at nets, or in the Taylors' driveway shooting baskets. Sam didn't hide out.

Then suddenly she knew. 'Thompson's wood,' she cried.

Matt's eyes narrowed.

'You know the place. A year or so ago, Sam and some friends built a fort in those woods.'

Matt's eyes grew bleak. 'Thompson's wood is huge. At least, it used to be. I would have thought by now it would have been parceled up into housing blocks.'

'Thompson died and bequeathed the woods to the city on the understanding they leave it intact.'

'In our day that's where kids went to get into trouble.'

'That's still where they go.' Jenny felt

new panic. 'Which is why I told Sam he couldn't go there anymore.'

'What makes you think he'd go there now?'

'We're out of possibilities. I don't know where he is. I just know he's not where he should be. At home. With me.'

'With us,' Matt corrected.

'Is there an us?' She hadn't thought herself able to talk about this yet, had been in stunned shock since the news on the radio, but now that her heart had recognized her love, the sooner they were clear about where they stood, the better. For she needed to get over the feelings she'd never lost; of desire, of longing, and of love.

'For Sam's sake, there had better be,' Matt growled.

'For Sam's sake, we had better find him then.'

Matt gazed at her hard. 'For our sakes too. You can't run from what's between us, Jenny.'

'It's not me doing the running.' She turned away. 'Let's just get going.'

245

She could feel him behind her, but didn't look back. If she let him near, she'd again be lost, unable to live without him by her side.

They ran for the car through the driving rain, the water beating off the pavement and drenching their shoes. Jenny couldn't even think of how Sam might be faring. He'd be soaked to the skin out in the cold, wet night. With his asthma, the stress . . . her heart clenched in her chest.

'He'll be all right,' Matt said again, seeming to know what she was thinking. 'We're going to find him.' Matt opened Jenny's door. 'Get in,' he ordered.

*   *   *

The woods were darker and thicker than Jenny remembered. Except for the road that cut through one side, the only other paths were barely visible. The woods were only a mile from their home. Sam could have run here before

Matt had looked beyond a few blocks' radius.

She wanted to find him, but she didn't want to find him here, in this dangerous place in the dead of the night.

'Pull over there,' she directed Matt, pointing to a faint trail on their right.

'Is that the path? It's so overgrown!'

'I think it's the one Sam and his friends made.' Jenny's stomach rolled. 'Although it's been so long since I've been here, I'm not sure. I remember we had to cross a stream, but that was in the woods a little way.'

Matt's frown deepened as he stared at the water streaming down their windshield. 'You'd better stay in the car.'

She grabbed the door handle. 'You don't know where you're going.'

He took hold of her arm and stopped her. 'Why can't you just do as I tell you?' And why did her skin have to feel like satin?

She stared back at him, her blue eyes

turning black. 'Sam's my baby, Matt.'

'I'll get him for you.'

'If you were me, would you stay behind?'

He released a gust of air. 'All right,' he said. 'We'll go together.' Slowly, reluctantly, he took his hand away, fearing that when he did, the night would suck her up.

She twisted the handle and stepped out into the maelstrom, her hair whipping forward over her eyes. Within seconds the rain had drenched her body, her dress and sweater clinging like a second skin.

Sam would be this wet, and cold to boot.

Matt joined her around her side of the car, longing to hold her, to keep her safe. All light from the stars and moon were blocked by the clouds. The flashlight Matt held showed pencil thin along the trail.

A trail that petered out after ten yards.

Matt turned to Jenny. 'Are you sure

this is the way?'

'Yes,' she said, her hand stealing into his.

Matt squeezed it tightly then put his arm around her so they moved forward together.

It seemed impossible Sam could have come this way. Twigs caught their hair, weeds clung to their feet, and brambles hooked their clothes — impeding them, snagging them, threatening to trip them.

Suddenly, with a gasp, Jenny pointed to a bush. A swatch of red cotton clung to one of its branches as securely as a painting nailed to a wall. 'Sam's been here,' Jenny said, her breathing ragged. 'He was wearing a red shirt.'

Matt plucked the fabric from the branch and felt for a moment the thinness of the cloth. Reluctantly, he thrust the swatch into Jenny's waiting hand.

She rubbed it between her fingers, then glanced up at him, her eyes dark with fear. 'He must be freezing,' she said, her voice echoing his own fear. 'Come on. Let's get going.' She moved forward a few steps, then stopped at a cross path.

'Which way?' Matt asked. The path they were on was the width of a deer's foot, all right for a twelve-year-old, but more difficult for an adult. The other path was even narrower.

Jenny bit her bottom lip. 'I'm not sure, but I remember when Matt brought me here, we turned right after a big tree. That tree, I think.' She pointed to a towering fir. 'But all the trees look big, and it was during the day when I came here before.'

Even if the night sky hadn't been blocked by clouds, the blanket of branches would have blocked any light shed by stars. Only the rain made it through, catching on the branches and joining together to cascade down.

'This way,' Jenny said, making a decision and taking the trail to the right.

Matt swiped his hand across his face

in a vain attempt to remove the rain, then he pushed forward through the undergrowth, holding the branches aside for Jenny. 'Do you remember how far you walked from the road?'

'About twenty minutes.' Jenny frowned. 'But that was during the day. And it wasn't raining. It'll probably take longer than twenty minutes.'

Matt twisted his lips. 'It's been longer than that already.'

'Then we must be getting close.'

As though Jenny's words precipitated the sound, Matt suddenly heard the rush of running water. Not the tinkling music of a simple stream, but a muted roar that rumbled the earth. He tugged on Jenny's hand and they moved toward the sound.

What normally must have been a gentle current had been replaced with a flood, and on top of the flood raced branches and leaves, tumbling and turning their way downstream.

Matt glanced at Jenny, saw her eyes widen.

'The fort's on the other side.' She pointed with a trembling hand across the water. 'But how could Sam get across this stream?'

'The rain had just started when he ran away. It probably wasn't flooding then.'

Jenny shoved back the sleeve of her blue sweater and peered through the gloom at her Mickey Mouse watch. 'He's been gone for hours.' She looked back at Matt. 'All this water . . . so fast.' Her shoulders stiffened. 'It doesn't matter how much water. We have to get across.'

She took a step forward.

Matt grabbed her arm and pulled her back. 'Forget it,' he said.

'We've got to get Sam.'

'I'll get him,' Matt growled.

Jenny stared into his eyes.

'I love him,' he said.

15

Matt had never spoken those words aloud, but the minute he did, he knew they were true.

Jenny's lips parted then just as swiftly shut. 'We'll go together,' she declared softly.

Matt placed his arm around her shoulders, felt her warmth and her vulnerability. 'This time you have to listen. You need to stay here. If anything goes wrong, someone has to get help.'

She glanced at the water. 'It's dangerous,' she said.

'I'm tough,' he replied.

But the blue eyes meeting his were filled with fear. 'What if the current sweeps you away?'

'Then you'll phone for help.'

'You'd be long gone before help could ever get here.' Jenny's lips trembled as she spoke.

'Nothing's going to sweep me away.'

'What about a rope? Do you have one in the car?'

'No rope,' Matt replied.

'I don't like this,' Jenny said.

Matt's heart swelled at the unexpected tenderness in her voice, and how even in the storm Jenny's scent overtook him. It was like the storm itself, wild and fierce.

'Don't worry,' he said again. 'I'll be fine.'

'You don't know that,' she whispered.

'I know we have to get to him quickly. With this storm and the stress, there's no telling how he's coping.' Matt frowned. 'Should I take his puffer with me?'

'Leave it with me,' Jenny said. 'That current looks strong enough to pull off your shoes. It could easily pull the puffer from your pocket.'

Matt nodded, then turned and faced the stream. Before the water had risen, he could have scrambled down the bank, but now there was no way to see the best route.

He moved forward another step.

'How are you going to do this?' Jenny asked. 'You can't just jump in!'

'Do you see any other way?'

'No,' she said numbly.

'Sometimes jumping in is exactly what you have to do.'

Normally the water would have been a foot high, easy to cross on embedded boulders, or to splash through risking only wet feet. Now it had risen to overflow its banks and had expanded to a width of at least twelve feet. It was hard to tell where the creek bank began, but another few steps would solve that problem.

Somewhere on the opposite side lay his son, a boy he was only just getting to know. The thought of Sam in trouble turned Matt's body cold, more freezing than the rain still streaming off his body. The thought of Jenny also, worrying and afraid, made Matt want more than anything to have them both safe. He gave Jenny's hand a farewell squeeze.

How could Matt feel so warm, when her insides were frozen? How could he seem in control, when it was obvious they had none?

Jenny swallowed hard. For the past thirteen years, she'd struggled to keep her life together, to forget Matt Chambers and help her son grow up, to make Sam happy despite the fact he had no father.

Now, when she had least expected it, his father was here, and had dredged up emotions she'd thought were long gone. It didn't even matter whether he intended to stay in Seattle or leave again for somehow he had done what he had done before. He had stolen her heart and along with it her soul. She had tried with all her might not to let him do either, but somehow choice had disappeared from the equation.

Now he was about to throw himself into danger, and she couldn't stop him because Sam was in danger too. While she stood on a bank wondering if she'd ever hold either of them again.

Her heart caught as she watched Matt move toward the bank, slogging through inches of water. He glanced back once and smiled at her, managing, despite all odds, to instill her with faith that he would find Sam and bring him back safely.

Matt took hold of a bush poking out through the water then with another step was over the edge, sliding down the hidden bank into the current.

'Matt!' she cried, but her voice disappeared in the roar of water.

Matt dropped straight in and under the water, and for an instant she could no longer see him. Then just as swiftly as he had disappeared, he re-emerged, teetering for a moment as though searching for footing. He released the bush and paddled with his arms to combat the current.

Jenny caught her breath. He had to stay upright. If Matt fell over, he'd be swept away. The current was doing its best to tug him downstream, while the branches racing by snagged at him . . . pulled.

Jenny reached down and touched the water, praying it wouldn't be as frigid as it looked. The cold lapped her hand and spread up her arm. Her body turned to ice at the mere thought of being immersed.

Matt was now barely visible, was simply a black shadow against the water's surface, hidden by the night and streams of falling rain.

'Matt!' she cried again. If he fell, she might not even know it.

She heard a sound as though he called back, but the wind caught his words and whipped them away before she could decipher them. At least his head was still above water, and he appeared to be almost half way across. How on earth was he going to get up on to the other bank? It must be as slick and muddy as this one.

She took a step closer, straining to see, then just as swiftly stepped back again as her foot felt the bank's edge.

She couldn't fall in herself, or she wouldn't be there when Matt needed help.

Jenny stared at the water and felt slightly nauseous, then averted her eyes so as not to see its flow. She would keep her gaze on Matt, not watch the water's current. She could see his head and shoulders nearing the other side. He stretched and reached for a dangling bush that rose like a sentinel from the water's surface.

It didn't appear to be attached to anything, or strong enough either to bear Matt's weight, but he grabbed on to it nonetheless and let his legs float up. The current pushed his body, tried to sweep it downstream, but Matt held on to the bush and slowly, surely, edged his body over the bank.

The shallow overflow water where Matt lay must be filled with mud and debris from the flood, but it didn't have the power of the water in the middle. Jenny's breathing eased when she saw Matt stand.

He was safe. Her heart sang. Then the old fear swept in. Would Matt be able to find her son?

★ ★ ★

'Sam,' Matt hollered, aware that with every step water squelched from his shoes. When he glanced back toward Jenny, he could scarcely see her. He wished there was some way to reassure her, but he was far from reassured himself.

Sam must be close by if he had come across the stream, as there was no way he could have made it back. But in what condition would he find the boy? And if his son was sick, it was his fault, for he had filled Sam with stress and caused him to run away.

He had to find Sam. For Jenny. For himself.

'Sam!' he cried again.

It was so damned dark. If he wanted to stay lost, the kid had come to the right place. Then a sound emerged from out of the darkness, like the barking of a fox gone to ground. It came again, followed by a choking noise.

'Sam,' Matt breathed, moving as fast as possible toward the sound.

He almost fell right on top of his son, for Sam was lying beneath a tree. His arms were wrapped around his body and his eyes were tightly shut.

His mouth was open, but the only sound emerging was a staccato coughing, and after the coughing an agonized wheeze, the horrid sound of lungs with no air to fill them.

The boy seemed to sense that Matt was there, for his eyes opened briefly and fixed on Matt's face. Sam's fingers were white as though from cold, while the rest of his skin was a pale shade of blue. The opposite hue of life-filled red. Sam needed medical help and fast.

Sam's eyes, when they opened, seemed dazed and unfocussed, as though he were on some hallucinatory drug, but Matt knew it was simply the struggle of Sam's body to get enough air into his lungs.

'Everything's going to be all right,' Matt said, in a voice as firm as he could muster. He could only pray the boy wouldn't be further stressed by the presence of the man he now knew to be his father.

Sam opened his eyes for a second time, and in their centers, Matt spotted relief. Then the rasping and choking noises began again.

Matt dropped to his knees and gathered Sam in his arms, felt a surge of joy to have found him at last. Then the boy's body went limp, and for one endless moment, Matt thought his son had died. He stroked Sam's arm and tried to warm him, wished he had a blanket with which to cover him.

'It's all right,' Matt said again urgently. 'I'll take you to your mother.'

Sam's eyes flickered as though he understood, but his cough grew worse. He lifted his hand and scrabbled at his throat, as though trying to relieve the pressure there.

Matt hugged the boy close to his body and tried to impart whatever warmth his own body still possessed. It couldn't be much, not after his icy swim, but it had to be more than Sam's reserves. The boy needed warmth and also oxygen, but most of all he needed medication to clear the passage to his lungs.

Matt prayed that when Sam saw his mother, her presence would give him some modicum of calm, would help soothe the difficulty he had in breathing.

Gripping Sam tightly, Matt gathered his sapped strength, and stood and made his way back toward the stream. Jenny was waiting on the other side, the sleeting rain still falling between them.

'Jenny,' he called.

Her silhouette moved, and for one heart-stopping moment seemed to come toward him. 'Go back,' Matt hollered, terrified again that she'd attempt to cross the river. She'd never make it. It had been hard enough for him. Getting Sam back across would be a challenge. 'Stay there,' he called. 'I've got Sam. I'm coming.'

He stared at the river, then at the boy in his arms, whose eyes were shut again as he struggled to breathe. This time he couldn't simply slide into the creek. The shock of the cold water would take Sam's remaining air. But no matter how he got down the bank, there seemed no way to protect the boy from the water. Matt brushed away the raindrops from his son's cheek and was rewarded when Sam again opened his eyes.

'Can you hang on if I put you on my back?' Matt asked.

The boy's gaze flickered to the racing current, and a cough racked his body, threatening to choke him. There was fear in Sam's eyes, but he slowly nodded.

Pride swept through Matt. The boy had Jenny's courage, for only a strong woman could have raised his son all on her own.

She wasn't on her own now. She never would be again. Not if he had anything to say about it.

With a twist of his body, he shifted Sam to his back and felt the boy's arms tighten around his neck. Then he turned his attention back to the creek.

Somehow he had to get into the river and do it this time without going under. The shrub with which he had pulled himself up would never hold the weight of two.

Perhaps if he turned and slid down the bank, he could hold on to the side for balance. It would take both hands. Could Sam hold on? He twisted his head to look at his son, but could barely see him. The boy's face was pressed against Matt's back and from his throat came the sound of shallow breathing.

'Sam,' Matt said. 'We're going in. Hold on tight.'

Sam eyes remained shut but his arms tightened around Matt's neck.

Matt pulled in a breath and turned away from the stream. With tiny steps, he moved cautiously backwards, dragging his toes across the ground before committing his feet to any spot.

When he reached the drop-off, he fell to his knees, feeling the water cover his legs. It had been cold the last time. Now it was freezing. But the sooner he got in, the sooner he'd be out. And the sooner he'd be able to get Sam to safety.

Sam lay along his back, his coughs rocking Matt's body, while Matt moved on his knees to the edge of the bank. Then taking a deep breath, he slid into the water.

The cold slammed into him and into Sam too, for the boy's grip became a vice. Matt spread his arms along the bank for balance and dug his fingers into the earth. He clung to that position as the current hit him, scrabbling on the creek bottom for a grip with his feet.

When he felt he had the measure of

the current, he slowly turned and faced upstream. Then he turned another ninety degrees and carefully made his way toward the opposite bank.

He struggled to keep from falling under while at the same time he pushed branches aside. They threatened to catch both him and Sam and drag them downstream or under the water. Sam's face was still pressed against Matt's back and his legs still clung to Matt's waist, but the boy's grip around his neck loosened.

Matt tried to move faster. He had to get to the far shore before the boy passed out. He glanced toward the sky, felt the rain on his face, but Jenny's silhouette was clearer now. He saw her once more move closer to the edge.

'Move back!' he shouted, but she ignored him, dropping to her knees and holding out her hand. She appeared as an island in the middle of the current, for the water overflowing the banks lapped her body. There was fear in her eyes but also determination.

He took another step and was finally close enough. He held out his hand, almost reaching her fingers. Then Sam shifted and upset Matt's balance. For an instant he thought his son would be torn away, but swiftly he twisted his arm around his back and pulled the boy's legs tight around his waist.

The river pulled hard, but Matt braced his feet, holding steady as the water swirled. All feeling in his legs had disappeared, but his arm muscles ached from clutching Sam.

One more step, then another and he'd be within reach of Jenny and of the bank and of safety for his boy. Matt gritted his jaw and managed that step, fighting the force of the current. Just when he thought he could go no further, Jenny's hand touched his shoulder.

He dared not take hold for fear the current would drag her in too. Sam was sagging against him now. He had to find the strength to get them both up.

'Give Sam to me,' Jenny cried, her

voice thin above the rain.

'You can't hold him,' Matt said.

'I can. I will.'

Matt stationed his feet against the current and slowly, carefully, eased Sam around. The boy's body seemed more limp than before as though he'd lost strength as the minutes passed. Matt braced himself against the bank, then as swiftly as possible heaved Sam into Jenny's arms.

She gripped him so tightly her knuckles turned white. Her face set and pale, she didn't try to rise, but instead pulled the puffer from her pocket and placed it between Sam's cold lips.

Matt did as before, allowing his legs to float to the surface then before the current could grab him and wrench him away, he eased his body up onto the bank.

He lay there a moment trying to catch his breath then, with a mighty push, rose to his feet. He took Sam back out of Jenny's arms and held him so the puffer wouldn't fall. Then he held out his hand and helped Jenny up.

'Are you all right?' he asked, wishing he could hold her, wishing he could wipe the cold from her body.

'Yes,' she whispered. 'Thank you,' she added softly.

He didn't want thanks. He wanted only Sam's safety, and from the sound of his son's labored breathing and the bluish pallor of the boy's skin, Sam was in as much jeopardy now as he had been on the far side of the stream.

He put one arm around Jenny's waist and pulled her after him along the path toward the road.

16

Sam's hand was still cold and seemed so small, not like that of a twelve-year-old boy at all. His body, too, seemed smaller in the big hospital bed than it did in his bed at home. Jenny enclosed his hand in hers and tried to transfer her warmth to her son's frozen body.

The nurses had placed a heated blanket on Sam and covered his face with a ventilator mask. Drugs to clear his lungs poured through the steam from the nebulizer at his side. With each passing minute, Sam's breathing grew calmer.

Lord only knew how he'd be when he woke up and remembered what had caused him to run away. Would the stress of that memory bring on another attack or had the ordeal he'd shared with his father brought them to an understanding?

Jenny shifted beneath the blanket a nurse had wrapped around her and glanced across the room to where Matt stood by the door. He was talking to the doctor, his dark gaze focused. She wanted to go and wrap her arms around him, to thank him again for what he had done. If he hadn't been there, hadn't rescued her son, she wouldn't be holding Sam's hand now.

Matt shot a glance in her direction, then swiftly smiled and turned back to the doctor. She couldn't turn away, couldn't pull her gaze from him, couldn't turn off the heat erupting in her heart.

She loved this man, had always loved him. She couldn't think now what she would do without him. When he returned to Miami, how would she survive? She squeezed Sam's hand and knew she would have to.

Matt appeared at her side. 'He's going to be all right.'

She knew that he would, but could

the same be said of her? Even Matt's voice sent her senses spinning, filling her heart with love and longing. How could she have let him batter down her barriers and then surge in and steal her heart?

'The doctor said Sam is making good progress, that he should be recovered within a few days.' Matt took his son's other hand. 'He's tough,' he said proudly.

Matt was tough too, but he was also gentle. The way he'd held their son while saving him was indelibly printed on her heart.

'How are *you* doing?' Matt suddenly asked.

She swallowed hard, wishing her breathing hadn't become like her son's; shallow, fast and altogether inadequate. 'Fine,' she replied, her heart beating too fast also.

'Have you phoned your parents?'

'No, I haven't.' Weariness engulfed her. 'I spoke to Vivian and she said she would call them.'

'Good,' Matt said softly. 'Sam needs his family.'

'Yes,' Jenny replied. But needing . . . wanting . . . weren't always enough.

'I found Coach waiting outside in the hall. He offered to go and get us some coffee.'

'Is the team here too?'

'I sent them home.'

Jenny couldn't believe the efforts Coach and the team had made scouring the streets to find her son. Coach might never say to her that he was sorry, but his actions spoke louder than his words ever could.

'We have to talk,' Matt said, breaking into her thoughts.

She tried to smile. 'Talking is what got us into this mess.'

'You're right,' he replied, his low, sexy voice filled with regret. Then he shook his head as though dissipating a fog, and took her hand in his.

She stared down at his fingers, saw their brown, strong lines, and knew that Sam had the same hands.

Sam's hand under hers. Matt's above. Only her hand kept the other two apart.

Fear spiraled through her. She had to know what Matt intended about the future. If he wasn't going to stay, she had to make him go, swiftly before she learned to love him even more and spend endless more years regretting her love.

Matt leaned towards her across Sam's bed.

'What was it you wanted to talk about?' she asked.

'Us,' he replied, his gaze locking on hers.

'Is there an us?' At that very instant, she felt Sam's fingers stir. Matt must have sensed the movement also, for he looked down at their hands and then at his son's face.

'Hey, bud,' he said softly, 'are you awake?'

Sam's eyes flickered open, then just as swiftly closed.

'Your mom and I are both here,' Matt went on.

'I don't think he can hear you,' Jenny said.

'I think he can.'

'I don't want him upset.'

Matt's eyebrows rose.

'You saw how he reacted when he heard you were his father.'

Matt swiped a hand slowly over his brow. 'It feels as though that was a lifetime ago.'

'Only a few short hours.'

'Sam and I have worked past that now.'

'Have you?' Jenny asked. 'Sam hasn't spoken a word to us yet.'

'He hasn't had the breath to speak, but I know he and I are going to be all right. He was glad to see me when I found him in the woods.'

Jenny squeezed Sam's hand. She couldn't meet Matt's gaze but she forced herself to say the words plaguing her heart. 'Of course Sam was glad. He knew how sick he was, knew he could die if he didn't accept help.'

'It was more than that.'

'How do you know?'

'The same way I know I love him and he loves me.'

Jenny's heart skipped. Matt had said again what he'd said at the river, the words she had longed to hear on the day their child was born. 'I know you love him,' she said quietly. 'If it hadn't been for you he might have died.'

'I have a lot to make up for.'

'This is twice now you've given me the gift of Sam. I can't tell you what that means.'

'You don't have to tell me.' Matt's gaze pierced hers. 'It means we need to stick together.'

Matt had said he loved Sam, and she could see it in his eyes, but he hadn't once said that he loved her too. Not since they were teens, not since he'd come back. They had made love in a frenzy of desire, and that had been wonderful, but if he took the job in Miami, all they had shared would be for nothing. She would have got burned resurrecting past flames.

She pulled her hand away and felt the loss of Matt's heat then, before she changed her mind, rose swiftly to her feet. She heard Matt call out as she left the room, but she forced her feet forward to get somewhere safe.

Once in the hall outside her strength suddenly left her. She leaned against a wall, tried to recapture her breath.

'Jenny,' Matt said, suddenly, miraculously, appearing beside her.

She longed to throw herself into his arms, but that would betray her own need and desire.

Slowly, gently, as though she was fragile, he pulled her around and held her tightly.

She couldn't think clearly enclosed in his arms, couldn't resist the lure of his warmth. All she knew was that she wanted his love, now and forever and for all time. If she couldn't have that, she didn't want him at all.

'We almost lost Sam,' Matt murmured in her ear. 'I don't want to lose you.'

She tilted her head, stared deep into

his eyes. 'Have we found each other now?'

His eyes, staring down at her, were steady and clear. 'Yes,' he said, smiling his slow smile.

'I want you in Sam's life — ' Jenny began.

'In your life too?'

She tried to ignore the tingling in her chest, tried to push aside what loving him was like. 'I'll let you see Sam.' She was determined to be fair. 'I want him to know what an amazing father he has. But — ' She took a breath. ' — that doesn't mean you and I have to be together.'

'Unless we want to be.' His arms tightened around her waist. 'And I want to be.'

'What about the coaching job in Miami? The radio said — '

'I don't give a damn what the radio said. They got it wrong.'

'So you're not moving?' She searched his eyes, determined to face whatever truth she saw.

'I have to be with you and Sam. No job even comes close to that.' He brushed his lips against her forehead, the heat of his kiss searing her skin.

She had feared the love she felt for this man, had feared the hurt their loving could bring. But suddenly she knew she had to trust, had to believe he wouldn't leave. With a long sigh, she released her fear.

'I want you,' she whispered.

'I love you, Jenny.'

Her heart began pounding a triumphant refrain, and joy sped in waves throughout her body. 'Are you sure?' she asked.

'Absolutely certain.'

Then before she could even draw a breath, he kissed her again and sealed their promise. She stood motionless, locked in his arms, the only sound the beating of her heart, and against that beat, the steady thumping of Matt's.

'Sam,' he went on, 'is only half of what I want.' He placed his hand beneath Jenny's chin and forced her gaze to meet his. 'You're the other half. Without you, I'm not whole.'

Then he kissed her again, in a way that thrilled, right down her body and into her toes.

'These last years have been hell,' he continued fiercely. 'No matter how much I tried, I couldn't forget you. When I thought of you married to somebody else . . .'

She traced his frown away from his eyes. 'I've never loved anyone like I've loved you.' It was such a relief to say that she loved him, to feel the weight lift as the words left her heart.

'And I was too stupid to know and believe that.'

'We both made mistakes.' She dropped a kiss on his mouth.

A long moment passed as he kissed her back, slow and spine-tingling and filled with emotion. 'A long time ago, I realized I loved you. I didn't care if your baby was mine.' He kissed her again as though he'd never stop. 'But by the time I figured that out, you were married and I was too late.'

'It's never too late.'

'I never want to lose you again.'

This time their kiss had the intensity of two storms, coming together with the promise of fine skies sweeping behind. It was fierce and then sweet, hard and then light, then fierce again in unspoken vows.

'I want you,' Matt growled. 'Now and forever.'

Forever. Jenny sighed. That was just about right. To love and to hold. Lord, how she was held. To care and be cared for, to honor and cherish. No simple words were enough to describe the emotion welling in her breast.

'We have a lifetime of catching up to do,' Matt said. 'And better yet, a future to create.'

'What sort of future?'

'One filled with you — '

'And Sam.'

'And a whole host of other little Chambers.'

'More babies?' she said, stunned at

the thought, stunned also by the joy overwhelming her. She smiled. 'What makes you think we're ready for more children?'

'You're the perfect mother.' Matt kissed her nose.

'I haven't felt so perfect lately.'

He pulled her close, telling her with his embrace that he thought she was. 'Sam's perfection is down to you.'

'Sam's not perfect either. You'll find that out.' But she would battle anyone who said he wasn't.

'I've got a lot of finding out to do.' Matt smiled as though that was just fine with him.

'Just love Sam,' Jenny said gently. 'That's all your son needs.'

'And you?' Matt asked, gazing into her eyes.

'That's all I need also.'

'Then it's easy.' He captured her lips for another long moment before finally, reluctantly, pulling away.

'I've told my mother about you and Sam. She can hardly wait to meet you both.' He gazed down at her with love in his eyes. 'She's been longing for a grandchild.'

'You've got it all planned.'

'Yes,' he said, then suddenly grinned. 'Sam can be my best man.'

'Best man?'

'When we get married.'

'Married!'

'What else?' His expression grew serious. 'Will you marry me, Jenny?'

It seemed as though in this hall, violins played, and the hospital's antiseptic smells were overlaid by the heady scent of perfume. She could have sworn she felt the swish of satin around her legs, and heard the tinkle of laughter and toasts with champagne. She saw in her mind's eye the heart on the tree at the edge of the cliff, encircling their initials with love and commitment.

'Yes,' Jenny whispered, her heart exulting.

'I love you,' Matt said again. 'And I'm going to spend the rest of my life showing you and Sam how much.'

'I do need someone to do the dishes,' she replied.

Matt chuckled. 'The dishes it is. I can wash. Sam can dry.'

'You're very certain.'

'I've never been more certain of anything in my life.'

'Sam's very protective. Don't forget he can throw rocks.'

'He didn't know me then, didn't know I loved you both.' Matt cupped her face between his hands. 'He knows that now. We've crossed rivers together. We're bonded for life.' Matt's lips lit on hers, brushing them with velvet. 'I can do rivers, but you're going to have to teach me the other stuff.'

'You're a natural,' she said, meaning it.

He kissed her again. 'Let's go back to Sam and see how he is. When he's better, we need to tell him everything.' Matt's eyes grew serious. 'We want no more secrets.'

'No more secrets,' she agreed.

'And maybe later, when Sam's

settled, you and I can take a little ride.'

'A little ride?'

'In the Chieftain.' Matt smiled again, even broader this time. 'Time we got to work producing a brother or sister for the boy.'

'Not all our children have to be conceived in the back seat of a car!'

'Not just any car.' He nibbled her ear. 'The Chieftain's the only thing my father gave me that he loved.' He moved from her ear to the tip of her nose. 'But I don't care where our babies are made. I just don't think I can wait until I get you home.'

Home sounded wonderful now that Matt was going to be in it. 'Patience,' she said, nuzzling his neck.

'I'm not good at patience.'

She smiled, felt the joy and hope for the future. 'I think you're going to be very good for Sam and me.'

'Not nearly as good as you'll be for me.' He put his arm around her waist. 'Come along, my darling, let's go tell Sam.'

We do hope that you have enjoyed reading this large print book.

Did you know that all of our titles are available for purchase?

We publish a wide range of high quality large print books including:
**Romances, Mysteries, Classics
General Fiction
Non Fiction and Westerns**

Special interest titles available in large print are:
**The Little Oxford Dictionary
Music Book, Song Book
Hymn Book, Service Book**

Also available from us courtesy of Oxford University Press:
**Young Readers' Dictionary
(large print edition)
Young Readers' Thesaurus
(large print edition)**

For further information or a free brochure, please contact us at:
**Ulverscroft Large Print Books Ltd.,
The Green, Bradgate Road, Anstey,
Leicester, LE7 7FU, England.
Tel:** (00 44) 0116 236 4325
Fax: (00 44) 0116 234 0205

A TEMPORARY AFFAIR

Carol MacLean

Cass Bryson is persuaded by her twin sister Lila to attend a celebrity party in her stead, accompanying the enigmatic photographer Finn Mallory. Then, when his secretary falls ill, he asks Cass to take over her job temporarily. Though she can't deny her attraction to her new boss, Cass is lacking in self-confidence, not least because of the scars she bears from a tragic accident. But Finn is drawn to Cass too, and it seems they might just find love together — until Lila returns, determined to capture his heart for herself . . .